1984

THE BLUE DANUBE

Also by Ludwig Bemelmans:

Now I Lay Me Down To Sleep

I Love You, I Love You, I Love You

Hotel Splendide

The Donkey Inside

Small Beer

Life Class

My War With The United States

LUDWIG BEMELMANS
The Blue Danube

**ILLUSTRATED
BY
THE AUTHOR**

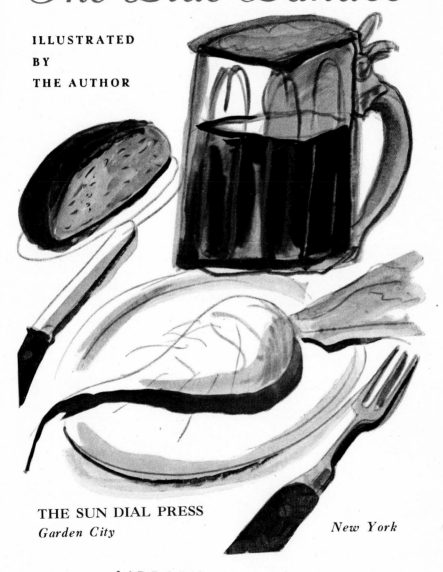

THE SUN DIAL PRESS
Garden City

New York

ILLUSTRATIONS

CHAPTER

1

Past flower-studded fields, past deep forests in which the pine trees stand in orderly rows, past clean villages and the stony fields of potato farmers, the Danube flows toward Regensburg.

The river comes to the city, swings in a wide arc past a flat terrain, once a grove shaded by linden trees and named after a German poet, "Die Schillerwiese." This wide field is now a municipal bathing establishment. In varying degrees of elegance, here stand the bath and boat houses of the club for the officers and wives of the Nazi Party. A respectable distance from that, the Danube bathes the noncommissioned personnel and minor Party officials. Adjoining this is the Schwimmverein of the common soldiers, ordinary Party members, and the police. The water flows on to bathe the civilian population, and eventually to a shallow moat in which the horses are washed.

After it has escaped the baths, the Danube is herded between two stone quays. The river is now a fast flowing mirror in which are reflected the two Gothic spires of the cathedral and an elaborate stone bridge that was built in the twelfth century, a landmark whose description takes up half a page in the Baedeker of South Germany.

The mirror breaks against the six stone buttresses of the bridge. Divided into five foamy rivers, the Danube roars out of the arches, its wild currents like a room filled with jostling, white-haired dancers.

That part of the Danube is called "the Strudel," and the women of Regensburg who threaten their husbands never say, like the Viennese, "I shall walk into the Danube." They say, "I will jump into the Strudel."

At a point two hundred yards past the bridge, the Strudel has, in years of ceaseless effort, built an island out of stone, silt, sand, and loam. Nameless and uncharted, its contours are forever changing, and in the floods of spring the twelve willow trees that promise it some permanence and seem to anchor it begin to tremble and most of the isle vanishes.

Day in and day out, the river is the color of watery coffee with too much milk. At flood times, it turns to yellow ocher. The Danube appears blue only in a faded mural that decorates the orchestra shell of the beer garden Zur Blauen Donau.

"Schweinerei," screamed Herr Stolz, a Gauleiter of Regensburg. He made himself well heard above the music of the three-piece orchestra which played behind him. He pointed at the small, grayish pork cutlet with his knife and fork. He pushed the plate, in one shove, toward his wife so that the small piece of meat almost hopped out of the dish. But before the poor woman, who saw meat rarely, who ate at home before they went out, and contented herself with a sip from his beer and an ersatz-buttered roll, could reach for a fork, he had retrieved the plate. He hammered at the edge of it with the knife and looked around.

"Frau Saltner," he shouted, as the waitress came to the table. "Frau Saltner, it is a disgrace and a Schweinerei to put a plate like this in front of me, to call this a portion of Schweinefleisch, and to charge one mark and fifty pfennigs for it."

"Please, Papa," said Frau Stolz, patting the left sleeve of the Gauleiter.

"Shut your mouth," he said to her. "This doesn't concern you. You have nothing at all to do with it."

The hands of his poor wife sank back into her lap, and with worried, devoted eyes, she looked at the Gauleiter's face.

"But, Herr Gau—" the scared waitress began to answer.

He shut her up with the knife held high. "Don't tell me again, Frau Saltner. Don't tell me again there's a war going on."

On such occasions, the music stopped. The Herr Gauleiter addressed himself to the beer garden, which was filled with those citizens of Regensburg who did not find themselves at the front or in concentration camps, who had enough substance, leisure, and license to contemplate the beauties of the bridge and its reflection, to count the smokestacks of the breweries, and to order a meal. Their digestion was helped along by the patriotic airs and the waltzes of the band and fortified by the broadcasts of the Ministry of Information.

Herr Stolz was about to begin a tirade on the black market when someone who was seated at one of the tables near the river, shouted:

"Ein Schwein!"

For a moment there was astonishment and silence, because at that moment the Burgomaster of Regensburg, a functionary conveniently afflicted with total deafness, elegant in top hat and with an umbrella held in clasped, gloved hands in back of him, wandered past on the stone quay outside the beer garden.

The man at the small table, a serious official in the Bureau of Taxation, shouted, "Nein, nein—a real Schwein," and he pointed up river.

On the mirror-like surface, in the middle of the Danube, a raft approached. It seemed like the roof of a barn, and on it sat a fat pig.

"Ein Schwein." "Ja, ja, ein Schwein." "Ein herrliches Schwein." "Ein wunderbares Schwein," said the crowd in the beer garden with respect and admiration.

The orchestra stopped playing in the middle of *The Blue Danube*. The violinist ran to the fence and pointed his bow. The occupants of the beer garden surrounded Herr Stolz, who, with napkin tied around his neck and knife and fork in hand, stood at the fence.

At the sight of the rosy traveler, all argument and position was forgotten. Frau Saltner, pointing at the Schwein, said, "Ist das nicht ein schönes Schwein?"

"Ja, das ist ein schönes Schwein," said the Herr Gauleiter dreamily.

"Back—stand back," shouted Policeman Umlauf on the left bank of the Danube, and on the right, Policeman Rummelmeyer held back an equal number of people who were following the pig's progress.

As Policeman Umlauf passed the beer garden, the Gauleiter brought him to attention. "Dummkopf, idiot,

why don't you do something!" he snapped. "Go get that pig."

The policeman saluted. He said, "But what should I do?"

"Jump into the water, you Ochs," shouted the Gauleiter. "Swim after it, drag it ashore—and report to me."

During the conversation, the pig came to the bridge, and it moved slowly. Policeman Umlauf saluted once more, obediently took off his shako with one hand and loosened the holster of his gun with the other, and ran. The crowd ran after him.

Ahead of them was the deaf Burgomaster with the umbrella swinging in back of him like the pendulum on a clock. He had come to the part of the quay where he habitually turned around and walked back.

At that point the quay narrows. It passes under the leftmost of the arches, along with the water. The arch is dark and dank and, while he could not hear the frightening roar of the water, the Burgomaster's nose was offended.

People on their way home are just the proper distance from the beer garden to relieve themselves in the protective shadows of the moist tunnel. As the Burgomaster always did, he sniffed the air, stopped, looked at the cathedral, at the sky, and at the bridge. He observed that it was crowded with citizens who had ignored the instructions of the police to keep moving. Their faces all hung out over the granite balustrade and some pointed down to the river. He slowly turned in the direction their hands pointed. He carefully adjusted his hat, placed the umbrella in his left hand, and shaded his eyes, but the moment he saw the pig, he suddenly lost all magisterial bearing. The distance between himself and it shrank rapidly. The half-clad policeman and the crowd were coming toward him. As fast as he could, the Burgomaster ran under the narrow arch. He kneeled on the slimy stones of the quay, placed the palm of one hand on its edge, and holding the crook of his umbrella out over the water, he tried to hook the raft.

The pig shot by. The Burgomaster overreached himself and fell into the river where he tread water and cried for help. Policeman Umlauf, a member of the Schwimmverein, removed his trousers. He stopped for a moment, searched his orderly mind until he had established the fact that orders from a Burgomaster came before those of a Gauleiter, and decided to let the pig go and come to the rescue of the head of the city.

The pig was dizzy. The raft turned and shifted from one whirlpool to the other. Eventually it came to the Island, where it touched land. A corner of it scraped up on the sand. The pig walked ashore as one coming home from a casual and frequently made voyage. It looked up at an old man and two women who stood there. It grunted and then followed a path.

The musicians in the beer garden removed the chamois brushes, which are extremely sensitive to moisture, from their green hats and put them into ersatz aluminum tubes.

The blue shadows that normally hover in the arches of the bridge came out and enveloped the whole structure, smudging the cathedral, the old houses, and the quays. Raindrops splashed on the river and the chestnut trees in the garden began to drip.

The old man on the Island in the Danube reached down into the water. The Burgomaster's umbrella had just been washed ashore. He picked it up, shook the water out of it, opened it, and held it over the two little old women who were his sisters, and they walked up the path which the pig had taken.

CHAPTER

2

THE Island on which the pig landed was a thorn in
the flesh of the Bureau of Taxation of the city of
Regensburg. It had ripped a particularly deep wound in
the hide of Herr Oberassessor Nebenzahl. He was afflicted with a kind of fiscal hemophilia on the subject.

To survey, to assess, to determine the boundary of a
place which disappears during part of the year; which has
no name, no address or telephone; which is off any policeman's beat, independent of garbage collection, street
cleaning, and, besides, without outlets for gas and elec-
tricity; which is, furthermore, not visibly connected with
this bank of the Danube or the other. In short, to credit
the existence of as irresponsible a piece of terrain as the
small isle in the Danube is nothing for the stomach of a
German official.

Before Oberassessor Nebenzahl filed the phlegmatic
opinions which he had written on this subject, and before
the Unterassessor in his office requisitioned a new file in
which to isolate this germ from the orderly properties,
the aid of the Burgomaster had been invoked. He ordered
the inhabitants of the Island to be summoned. Fischer,
Anton; Fischer, Anna; Fischer, Martha; and their niece,
Leni, dutifully appeared.

Before the Burgomaster, Oberassessor Nebenzahl attempted to scuffle them into an admission of ownership

of the Island. He played a game of forfeits with them, threatened them with dispossession, but there was nothing they had that anybody could possibly want.

"But what do you live on?" screamed the Oberassessor. "What are your means of support? Take it down," he said to the Unterassessor, and that one wrote:

"Two or three crops of radishes are raised on the Island, depending on the weather. They are brought to market in baskets made by Fischer, Anton, out of the branches of the Island's twelve willow trees. These radishes are transported in a flat-bottom boat, also made by Fischer, Anton, and operated by him. These radishes are sold at the door of the brewery and the beer garden Zur Blauen Donau, and the four inhabitants of the Island share equally in the proceeds." These proceeds were too low to interest even a German tax collector.

"Let them go," said the Burgomaster.

"Do you receive any other support?" asked the Oberassessor. The clerk wrote:

"Fischer, Anton, states that he, his sisters, and his niece have no other support, no property, bank or safe deposit."

The Burgomaster and the Oberassessor had a long conference over the beer table in the garden of Zur Blauen Donau. They agreed that the easiest way out was to decide that, as far as the city was concerned, the Island and its people did not exist. The conscientious Oberassessor moved his chair, turned his back on the Island, and the dossier of the Fischers went to sleep in the municipal archives of the town.

The four people found themselves outside the protection of the benevolent State. They were wholly dependent now on their faith in God and His sunshine, and in the short season in which they raised their superb, white beer radishes.

During the Island's inundation, the four people wandered. Anton Fischer pulled a hard, old hat down on his head with both hands, and with a stick in hand, set out, always ahead, with most of the baggage and a guitar on his shoulder. The others followed him, the two sisters in the costume of Bavarian peasant women—a black, forever-lasting fabric, sleek and shiny with wear, their hair covered with old satin kerchiefs, knotted at the nape of the neck, the tips hanging down the back.

The pilgrims always took the same route, once out of sight of Regensburg. At an elevation to the north of the city, they sat down on a large, flat, moss-covered stone, and took their shoes off. Old Anton stowed them away in his rucksack. The women looked for a while at the muddy, foaming Danube and wiggled their toes while old Anton looked at young trees and cut suitable walking sticks from the trees. Eventually, when he said, "All right, let's go," they all got up, shouldered their burdens, and disappeared silently into the secret forest.

They walked one after the other on a path of burnished pine needles, down into valleys that imprison all sound, up again past endless corridors of trees where their voices got lost. In clearings, in the warm waves of air that are scented with wild strawberry and hedgerose, they rested and talked low until Leni awakened out of her deep young sleep. They searched for mushrooms and herbs, they prayed, and walked on until the sound of axes, of

dogs barking and roosters crowing, announced the end of the forest.

They sat down again on a rock, or under some familiar tree, put their shoes on again, and walked toward the golden crosses on the steeples of churches and monasteries.

The annual pilgrimage took them to the wonder-working grotto of St. Anna in Kelheim; to the miraculous black Madonna of Altötting, whose silver altar is flanked by the urns that hold the hearts of the Kings of Bavaria; to the blessed waters of Donaustauf; and past all the small village churches that were along the way.

Opposite almost every church or cloister in Bavaria is a tavern with a shady garden in which chickens and geese share the tables with the guests. As long as people there do not talk and only eat and drink and sing old songs, their world remains as untroubled and as much the same as one can hope for.

In those cool gardens with the dusty road outside, Anton sang his songs and played his guitar.

The height of their pleasures was to drink a quart of brown beer together slowly, wiping the heavy foam from their mouths with the back of the hand, sitting back to rest their eyes in the green light that filtered through the chestnut leaves and contemplate the color of the beer, to eat the sour peasant bread and the early, snow-white, spring radish.

After the wet, scratchy leaves are cut away along with the top of the radish, it is sliced paper thin, but so that the radish remains intact, opened like a fan. It is then salted and left alone until water comes oozing out between the slices. When it has wept its last tear, then the radish is ready to be eaten.

The Island people tasted it as winegrowers do their vintages. They approached the radish with suspicion, inspected it to see whether the core was firm or furry, whether it was too flat, bit the tongue, or sent fumes up into the nose and forced tears into the eyes. They judged how it went with the beer of that region and how the beer compared with that of the brewery that supplied the Blue Danube beer garden in Regensburg. These all-important questions were discussed endlessly and with the use of peculiar local phrases and time-honored proverbs.

"I am in doubt of many things," said old Anton, "but of one thing I am absolutely sure, and that is that the beer and the radishes of Regensburg are the best in the world."

"And don't forget the geese of Reinhausen," said Saint Anna.

"Yes, and the geese of Reinhausen," answered old Anton.

Reinhausen is a small village on the left bank of the Danube, at the influx of the river Regen, where heavy Bohemian geese are raised.

"And the cheese from Donaustauf," said old Martha.

"Yes, and the cheese from Donaustauf."

"And the smoked hams of Obertraubling," said Anna.

"And the Regensburger Knackwurst—don't forget that," cried old Anton. "The world is beautiful," he said, and stopped on the hill above the last village. The wooden wheel of a sawmill turned in shallow water; it seemed to pass through a tub of buttercups.

On the way back, they began a homesick talk about Regensburg as if they owned an estate there, as if they were a thousand miles away from there.

"I wonder what the Danube has brought us this year," Anton said, as they came out of the forest on the south side and saw the city before them.

Old Anton took his hat off, pointed at the cathedral, at the Strudel, at the bridge and the Island. Their hands were folded silently in prayer and, as they got their boat, which was left with a farmer in Reinhausen, and pushed out into the Danube, old Anton rowed hard, sang, and pushed over toward the Island.

CHAPTER 3

BEHIND the steady guardians of the Island—the twelve willow trees that were named after the Apostles—at the beginning of May the spine of a hill appeared. The gurgling of the Danube changed to a steady murmur and the wild waters parted under the tottering house and barn. The stilts on which they stood dried slowly in the oblique rays of the sun, and the air was filled with a lukewarm, slimy stench as the Island emerged from the floodwaters. The reeds, bushes, and grasses straightened themselves in a week's time. The low branches were weighed down with sleeves of mud and the tops of the willow trees were crowded like a junkman's cart with old shoes, strips of clothing, small firewood, empty bottles, sacks and other usable things. In one profitable spring, a buggy was caught there, and a butcher's meatgrinder that was attached to a table top.

The Islanders returned from their pilgrimage, looked to see if the house was still there, took their shoes off, and squeezing the warm ooze through their toes, silently wandered over the Island, stacking up the driftwood and digging for objects that had buried themselves in the mud.

While the Island was being cleared of this debris, it took on form. It declared its position and boundaries for that year. It was, at times, longer or wider, more upriver or down, and sometimes higher than it had been in other

years. The first few days it stank and the water ran off
it in a hundred small brooks. Then the loam cracked in
the patterns of broken glass. It was bleached to a pale
mustard color, and after two weeks of good weather, it
was dry as the Sahara.

There was as much work for the women as for the
man. The insides of eight large beer barrels were smeared
with pitch. With their tops removed, they were rolled
out and half buried, thirty feet apart, in one straight line
down the center of the Island. They were connected to a
pump by wooden gutters. After that the radish seed was
carefully paid out between thumb and index finger, three
seeds a foot apart, laid in a shallow trench and covered
with loose earth. From then on, the radish crop had to
be thoroughly watered twice a day. But toward evening,
when the red sun sank between the steeples of St. Ulrich's
Church·and the smokestack of the Emslander Brewery,
work stopped on the Island.

The sisters came out of the house, wearing black
knitted shawls, and sat down on the bench, close to the
pump. Folding their arms, they looked at the swallows
perched on four strands of telephone wire like black
notes on bars of music. Leni washed the dishes in cold
water while old Anton sat with his back toward his sisters
to keep the smoke of his pipe away from them, and
watched the white marble of the Walhalla blush until it
seemed that the temple was made of glowing coals.

The excursion train that runs from Regensburg to the
Walhalla whistled then, and they heard the screech of its
wheels as it went through an underpass. The lights of the
locomotive shone a while later as it slowed down to

pass through Reinhausen. The pig jerked his ears a while later at the squeal of the train entering Stadt am Hof, the sister city of Regensburg, across the river. Soon after that, the pig was locked up for the night. Leni threw dishwater into the Danube, and the people said good-night to each other and went to their beds.

On the evening after the planting, old Anton got the pump ready. He walked to the barn and carried out a ladder. It was the same every year. There was cool evening air moving along over the Danube, and as he brought out the ladder, he always told the same story. He pulled his hat down over his head with both hands, he leaned the ladder against one of the Apostle trees, and when he was half-way up, he said, "This reminds me of a story. Did I ever tell you the story of the farmer and the parrot? Listen, Leni. Once there was a poor German farmer and he had a large tree. One day a bird with glorious plumage flew overhead and sat down on one of the branches of the tree. It was a parrot, but this farmer had never seen a parrot. He got a ladder out of his barn and leaned it up against the tree and then climbed up to catch the bird. He was all the way up, almost touching the bird, when the bird said, 'Hello.'

" 'Oh, excuse me, sir, I thought you were a bird,' said the farmer, took off his hat, and meekly climbed down the ladder again."

Old Anton then took out his knife and cut the young reeds from the Apostle trees and collected the laughter for his story.

He had constructed a curious pump, one that survived the floods. It was his own invention, made of half an old

telegraph pole that had been washed ashore. Near the top of this was attached a small platform, and from the platform his two sisters stepped onto a board attached to the top of the pole, like a seesaw. By alternately going one step forward and one back, they worked the pump. Below them, the water flowed into the wooden gutters and down to the barrels where old Anton and Leni plunged heavy watering cans into the barrels and carried the water to the plants.

It took most of the day to fill the barrels. The sisters, Anna and Martha, hanging onto the rail, sailed up and down in the cool breeze that rides over the Danube. They enjoyed the view of the Island, of the city and the Danube.

They were both thin as rabbits but with the peasant's many underskirts and stiff clothes they seemed fat and heavy. Going up and down, they trailed the two tips of their black kerchiefs through the air. It gave the appearance of two black birds sitting in their hair, one descending on it, one about to fly up and away.

The appearance of the old sisters on their pump afforded a peculiar entertainment for the citizens of Regensburg. From the quay on which the Regensburgers promenaded, they appeared to be bobbing out of the roof of their house. Nursemaids pointed them out to their children as witches that were practicing on broomsticks.

The teacher of natural history once a year stopped his entire class on its morning walk and, pointing to the Island, used it as a primitive model to explain the life of the early lake dwellers.

On every day of the week mothers and children, slow-

promenading women who were expectant mothers, and quick-moving girls who worked in war factories, the twenty-six shadow-walking licensed prostitutes of Regensburg, and even the nuns, who usually walked with downcast eyes, glanced at the Island, as well as bakers, cobblers, Gauleiters, servant girls and soldiers—even the Bishop of Regensburg. At one time or another every citizen stood and looked at the Island. Some saw it as a palm-fringed, faraway place to which they would like to escape; some, like the Oberassessor Nebenzahl, were upset by its existence; Frau Saltner, like others, waved greetings to the inhabitants as she crossed the stone bridge on her way to work in the beer garden. It was there as prominent as the cathedral and the bridge. It was like a ship slowly moving upstream, with waves at the bow where the Apostle trees stood, and a placid, pale mass of deep quiet water at its stern.

On Sundays, the people of the Island were up hours before daylight. Their chores were done as the bells of St. Emeram called for early mass. They came with their prayerbooks and walked to the boat.

Old Anton placed a basket of freshly washed radishes in the boat. The two women stepped after him and sat down at the end. For the length of the Island, on the side where it was sheltered from the currents of the Strudel, he punted upstream, and then he pushed the boat out into the Danube. In crossing, the river carried it far below the point from which they had started.

Saint Anna walked to the cathedral. This great, Gothic church is drafty and wet like the sweating hold of an old ship, and at that early hour it is lit up by the little flickering lights of old women. They all have peculiar candles which they bring with them: a thin kind of waxstring, rolled up like a ball of wool, that lasts them for months and is called "Wachsstöcklein." They unwind a little of it every day, straighten a few inches, and light up their prayerbooks with it.

While Anna was in church, Martha was with old Anton, who carried the radishes over the stone bridge to the other side of the Danube to the brewery and the beer garden Zur Blauen Donau. There they established themselves at the right of the passage which leads through the brewery to the beer garden.

The garden was raked by a halfwitted boy. Sparrows quarreled under the legs of tables and chairs, and in the wooden music shell, on which the panorama with the very blue Danube was painted, Frau Saltner, in a starched apron and elaborate hairdress, filled salt and pepper shakers.

Old Anton was a little untidy in the clean morning stillness. He stood about for a while and then walked down the quay with his old pipe hanging out of his beard. He watched the sky, which is seldom free of clouds, the gentle landscape, the frugal beauty of the gray bridge and of the stone city. He admired the elegant equipment of the fishermen who sat along the quay with patience, a can of worms, and a license shield, and whom no one had ever seen walk home with a fish.

At ten the sisters changed guard and Martha went to church while Anna sat with the radishes. For good measure, Leni was taken to church by both of the devout sisters.

The musicians arrived and the clientele. The beer began to foam into the steins. Frau Saltner was warm and lost her smile. Hats were raised, compliments thrown. Gallantries flew through the air and heels were clicked to the strains of Strauss. The beer garden was animated with the brotherhood of German man; Oberassessor waved at Oberassessor, Major saluted Major, and baker shook the hand of butcher. Little boys whose ersatz rubber toy balloons exploded began to cry as hard as if they were good balloons.

After the music stopped, when all the radishes were sold and the garden emptied, old Anton walked in and quietly sat down at a table. He unpacked three extra fine radishes, sliced and salted them carefully, ordered a stein of beer and some black bread. While the radish wept, he waited for his sisters, and, looking again at the city, was thankful for his fate and said to himself that from where he sat he could see everything that was necessary to a good and sensible life.

CHAPTER
4

THE flicker of the Wachsstöcklein that stood before the little women in black shawls warmed a corner in the dark, drafty vastness of the cathedral.

A coughing sacristan lit six candles on the altar of St. Emeram, patron saint of Regensburg. A small bell rang and a priest and his altar boy came to celebrate Low Mass.

Frau Stolz prayed ardently, the bloodless fingers interlocked as in a cramp, the eyes closed and the lips moving. But at the earliest moment at which she could leave, she got up, hurried to a side portal, and ran through the Kapellenweg, through another narrow street that is called "The Beautiful Opportunity," down to the Danube. There, opening a heavy oaken door carefully, she entered a gabled house. A maid, a peasant girl with thick, dark eyebrows, in heavy felt slippers, went back through the corridor of the house. When Frau Stolz was seated at the breakfast table, the maid knocked at the Gauleiter's door and said,

"The coffee is getting cold, Herr Gauleiter."

"Ih kimm shoh," he answered. "Ih kimm shoh, Kathl."

"Ih kimm shoh" is not Chinese or Afghanistan, but the dark, grumbling Bavarian patois for the German, "Ich komme schon," which means, "I am coming already."

Frau Stolz, in her black dress, her hands folded, waited to pour out the morning coffee.

"Kimmt er?" she asked the maid.

The girl curtsied and pulled up the Gauleiter's chair. "Ja, ja, er kimmt shoh," she said. They both waited.

The animal with the voice sat up in bed and began to scratch through the heavy underwear, under the arms, the stomach, and then, sitting up and yawning, the nails went through the hair on his legs. The bed creaked. For a while the Gauleiter enjoyed the small, lustful pleasure that he derived from rubbing his index finger between his toes. He sat for a while on the edge of his bed, cleared his throat, and then stood up to stretch himself. He was five foot eight and weighed two hundred and fifty pounds: the perfect Party boss, with a broad, heavy skull, whose anatomy was as simple as a stone—its foremost organ, the mouth, attached by one thick chord to the Party brain, with no cool restroom, no clearing house for thought between; two simple lines that ran like the outline of a barrel from ears to ankles, a skeleton of heavy bones bedded in fat. His backside resembled two donkeys leaning against each other.

He was accomplished with knife and fork and the raising of the arm to the proper salute. He could pound and slap with one or both fists, and the sly, pig eyes were familiar with the sights of a rifle, a gun, or a pistol. Most highly developed were the muscles that pressed his buttocks together when he stood at attention before a superior.

The Gauleiter stepped from the room which smelled of him, his bed, his underwear, and the greased boots, into the narrow corridor that led to his store and the adjoining living room. As he entered, he acknowledged the greeting of his wife and sat down to unfold his copy of the *Stürmer*. While he read this inspiring publication with lips moving as ardently as his wife prayed, all else dropped from his ken.

This solemn silence was disturbed by the sound of the bell which was attached to the door by which customers entered the dry goods store of the Gauleiter from the street.

"Ih kimm shoh," shouted Herr Stolz through the curtain which divided the store from the living room.

He finished a poem, pushed his coffee cup away, put down the *Stürmer*, and searched with his feet for the felt slippers under the table. He moved the curtain aside and said a polite tradesman's good-morning, for which he was sorry a moment later, because the customer who waited for him in the store was old Anton.

As all things, so the language that is used between salesperson and customer in Germany is strictly regulated. It is as precise as the phrases one learns out of guidebooks to a foreign country.

Normally, the person behind the counter looks at the customer with deference and says, "What may I serve the lady or the gentleman?" or "What does the lady or the gentleman desire?" While the customer addresses the salesperson in the second person, the clerk continues to answer in the third.

Herr Stolz leaned over the counter, the weight of his body spreading the fingers of both hands, and he said,

"What do you want here?"

"I would like to buy something," said Anton.

"Oh," said Herr Stolz, and folded his arms.

"A handkerchief, I would like to buy."

"The gentleman wishes a handkerchief, a gift, perhaps?" said Herr Stolz, smiling.

"Yes, for a gift, for my niece," said old Anton.

"May I show the gentleman something in silk?"

"Yes, thank you," said Anton.

"Something colorful, perhaps, for the young lady?"

"Yes, that would be nice. Thank you very much."

Herr Stolz took a drawer and placed it on the counter. His wife came into the room and slipped behind the cashier's desk and looked at her husband. The Gauleiter searched among the pieces of cloth. He picked one out and held it up.

"Something red for the gentleman, perhaps?" he said, and, looking past Anton at his wife, he said loud and slowly, "Something red for the Bolshevist swine?"

"Papa, please," said Frau Stolz.

"They live on roast pig, Mama, and they've stopped blowing their noses into their fingers and wiping them on their sleeves. They need fancy handkerchiefs while the decent citizen who pay taxes and has sons in the field, if he buys a handkerchief at all, must buy one that has a black border."

The old man was silent. He turned and was about to go.

"Oh, don't go yet," said Herr Stolz. "What would the people think if it got around that we didn't take care of our customers? Here it is, take it. There's nobody in this town besides you who would. I'll let you have it very cheap."

"I've changed my mind. If I bought one I'd need one

with a black border, larger than any you have," said old Anton.

"And whom would you weep for?" said Herr Stolz.

"Deutschland and the Führer," said old Anton, and walked past him.

The Gauleiter ran into the street after the old man, and shouted,

"That is exactly what I have been waiting to hear from you.

"Mama, you heard what he said!" screamed the Gauleiter back toward his shop.

Old Anton walked quietly to the stone quay. He pulled his boat up to the point from where he always set off across the Danube. The wild currents of the Strudel carried him back, past the store.

The animal with the voice was at the quay. The pig eyes were bloodshot. Vexation, offense, and scandal hammered in his skull. He waved his fist.

"Bolshevist swine," he yelled. "You hang on a thin string. Wait and see. I'll teach you."

The boat passed him.

"I have never spoken to him. I kept away from all of them. I have attended to my own business, and now it has come to me. I knew it would come. It took a long time, but now it is here and it has touched me, too, and God knows how it will end," said Anton to himself, and made the boat fast.

CHAPTER
5

THE animal with the voice appeared in the city hall square an hour after old Anton had rowed back to his island. He had thrown himself into his Sunday uniform and between his eyebrows was the vertical wrinkle with which he signaled his importance to the world and which he wore when he was in that particular uniform, or in possession of a Party secret. He returned the salute of the sentry at the door of the city hall and entered the wing which was given over to the Bureau of Security. The sound of the impact of his boots along the stone-paved floor echoed ahead of him in the vaulted corridors and washed against the heavy oaken doors until he abruptly stopped, executed a right face, and opening the right door, approached a man so like himself that Gauleiter Stolz might have been looking into a mirror.

After a snappy Party greeting and a handshake with Gruppenführer Schuft, Herr Stolz was shown a seat. The Gruppenführer continued what he was doing, while Herr Stolz recited what he knew and suspected of Anton Fischer. In this room all the secrets of the citizens of Regensburg were on file. Gruppenführer Schuft saw that he hoped to find information that would round out the case against Fischer, Anton, and the people of the Island.

The obliging colleague interrupted his work and got up from his desk and walked to the rows of files. He

opened several envelopes, but there was nothing for or
against Fischer, Anton—there was no file on Fischer,
Anton. The officials looked at each other. "Also," said
Gauleiter Stolz, "that is the most slovenly thing I have
ever heard." The other shrugged his shoulders. "That is
the end of the world, of everything," said Herr Stolz.
Gruppenführer Schuft went back to his desk and continued checking some names against a list. "I will be
with you in an instant," he said, "but I must have this
ready when he comes—the Herr Hauptmann Trost from
Dachau, a fine man—" He held a batch of letters in his
hand, and in a low conversational tone read the familiar
names of a dozen Regensburgers off the envelopes,
counted them, checked them once more, and then, just
as he had finished and placed a band around the letters,
the door opened and the Gruppenführer jumped from
his chair and pressed his buttocks into respectful rigidity.
A tall, dark-skinned officer entered. He wore a black uniform and a cap, also black, to which was attached the
insignia that in other lands is found on the labels of
bottles containing poison.

The captain surveyed the room with military precision.
Automatically he checked the occupants' insignia and
searched for the ranking man. He executed a sharp left
turn, raised his arm in salute to the Gauleiter, and only
then, after that salute was returned, did he take cogni-
zance of the Gruppenführer. He made a right turn and
waited until Herr Schuft stood at attention and saluted
him, before acknowledging his presence with a return
salute.

Herr Schuft went over the list with the officer, who

said simply "Twelve today." He put the envelopes in the outside pocket of his coat, smoothed the flap down, and slapped his pocket several times to smooth it out. "The usual notifications to the relatives," said the tall man; he saluted, about-faced, and strode out. During the captain's visit, Herr Schuft had relaxed only when he reached for the envelopes and the list of names, whereupon he had immediately resumed the position of attention which he maintained throughout the time the officer was present.

After he had gone, the Gruppenführer looked after him through the door for a while and listened until the tramp of his boots was gone. "If only they were all like this one," he said to the Gauleiter, who had remained at ease and seated in a chair, "then things would be right. A fine man, the Herr Captain Trost from Dachau."

They both admired the order, the impersonal, casual, efficient process with which twelve Regensburgers who had talked too loudly and too carelessly—or had written through the wrong channels—were dealt with. In the twelve small manila envelopes which the captain had carried away in his coat pocket were their mimeographed death certificates.

"That is all he ever says," said Gruppenführer Schuft, " 'Ten today' or 'Twelve today,' and as he leaves he says, 'The usual notifications.' "

They felt let down after he was gone. On the desk was the folio in which they had looked in vain for the record of Anton Fischer. It took a while of talking and a rehashing of what had happened before they were sufficiently

aroused to consider the case of the Island as the menace
to the security of the State that it was.

"Our first move in the case of Fischer, Anton," said
Gruppenführer Schuft, "is to go to the Bureau of Taxation. They always have something on somebody when
no one else has. Come." This office was in a sprawl-
ing building near the Danube at the side of the stone
bridge, next to the tower.

The officials arrived at the office of Herr Oberassessor
Nebenzahl, and lost an hour there. The Oberassessor was
a stubborn, squareheaded, old-fashioned official who, in
years of service, had rubbed his cloth on the same desk.
This piece of furniture faced a window from which the
Danube and the Island could clearly be seen. Oberassessor Nebenzahl climbed a ladder and blew the dust from
the file which concerned itself with the Island and its
inhabitants. He was interrupted several times as he read
the official decision in the case. He showed the signature
of the Burgomaster and the official stamp of the magistrates of Regensburg at the end of the document, and he
pointed at it whenever the two Party officials demanded
that he do something about it. He explained the fiscal
dilemma several times, first in heated words, and then
slowly as if talking to children. He stated that consider-
ing everything, the city was fortunate because the three
people on the Island by right were entitled to old age
pensions, and would fall on the public purse if their
means of support were taken from them. When they
screamed at him, he screamed back, told them that there
was nothing that could be done about it. As far as he was

concerned the Island did not exist, neither did the people on it, and that was the way it was, and written and sealed—and disposed of. Finally he told them to get out of his office.

Outside on the stairs the Gruppenführer said, "That has not happened to me before—to be ordered out of an office—not since the Party came to power. The man is incapable of logic."

"We shall see," said Stolz. "Who is not for the State is against it. Nebenzahl better watch out. The Herr Oberassessor will not exist much longer either, unless he sees things in a very new light. He'll join those on the Island, I promise you!"

The two officials ran back to the office from which they had come, and immediately looked into the file of Oberassessor Nebenzahl, but, like Anton Fischer, he was hard to catch—he was Aryan, had three sons in the army, and was a Party member; there was nothing against him. They dictated a memorandum on their conversation with him and issued orders that he be watched, but beyond that there was little they could do to him except to relieve him of office, cashier his pension, and see that he was dropped from membership in the Party as lukewarm and reactionary. He seemed to have joined only under pressure, anyway, said the secretary of the local cell.

Altogether different—a man whose equipment, background, and Party history recommended him ideally for the job—was a candidate sponsored by Gauleiter Stolz. The ardent Party member, Robert Unruh, was a degree lower in the official stratification of the officeholders of the city; he was merely an assessor and attached to the

Bureau of Investigation, but he had valuable experience and was a man of the right heart and hand for the job. He had been one of the first to join the Party, fought in the streets of Nuremberg and Munich. He was distinguished by a scar inflicted by a chip from a flying seidel which had hit him at an explosion in a Munich beer cellar. Besides all this, Party member Unruh gave of his time freely. He was an air-raid warden and stood his watches up on the tower overlooking the bridge. The rare man was also talented, and in his few free moments wrote poetry which appeared regularly in the pages of the *Stürmer*.

After he had replaced a cheap oilprint of the Führer with a genuine, personally dedicated photograph and officially taken possession of his new office, Assessor Unruh gave proof that he, with all his gifts, was also a practical man. At the precise moment when the lukewarm, retired Oberassessor Nebenzahl, seated in the twilight of his living room, had finished contemplating whether he should press the muzzle of his revolver against his temple or shoot upwards through the roof of his mouth, and had come to the part of the tragedy where he stood before his mirror pointing his service revolver at his temple, the poet rang the doorbell. The Oberassessor placed the weapon on the table and went to open the door.

The visitor came to the point immediately. He measured the Oberassessor's girth and height with his eyes, said "Good evening," and without taking the offered seat, he casually inquired whether Herr Nebenzahl's uniform was for sale. "It must be almost new," he said. "You rarely wore it, Herr Oberassessor. Anyway you won't miss

it, you won't need it any more, and I can use it," he
added with clearest logic. It was a good uniform, cut of
cloth no longer obtainable. The boots proved somewhat
loose in the shafts, but were as little used as the cloth.
The retired officeholder released them, together with the
uniform, without a struggle and at the price which his
successor offered. The poet also bought the pistol, the
holster, the uniform cap was thrown in, and he took it
all along. In the frame of the door, the departing Unruh
rendered a stiff salute, to which Herr Nebenzahl, whose
life had been saved at the last moment, answered limply
like a fallen bird who tries to lift an injured wing.

After a period of rearranging furniture, disposing of
routine matters, listening to his immediate superiors getting his staff reoriented, Assessor Unruh felt sufficiently
at home to go to his beer garden. The Gauleiter asked
him what if anything had been done about the lord and
ladies of radish island. Assessor Unruh reported that he
had made a minute search in the archives of Regensburg
and had unearthed nothing new concerning the Island.
Legally, it still did not exist, and the resourceful man
proposed to leave it that way.

There were simpler ways of getting at the people on
the Island, he told Gauleiter Stolz. There was the Bureau
of Licenses, for example. His logic came into play—did
not every article made have a label "made in Germany,"
"made in Italy," "made in Japan?" Let the Bureau of
Markets issue licenses to peddlers, let there be a space on
the application for the license in which you fill in where
the produce is grown. "Look, Herr Gauleiter," he said,
"it's very simple." He submitted a loose sketch of the

proposed peddler's license. "Let them see whether they can fill that out. Question thirty-two asks: 'Where is the produce grown?' On an island that doesn't exist? Question thirty-three: 'By whom?' By people who do not exist? The answer is: 'No license.'"

"But if they get around it somehow?"

"Then," said the Assessor, hitting the table and raising his voice, "then we will issue a simple order that people who pick their noses and whose name is Fischer don't sell radishes in front of this beer garden, or any other beer garden—finished."

The Gauleiter looked with admiration at his protege. "We should have done it long ago—that way," he said, encouraged by the straightforwardness of the Assessor. "No more coddling."

They clinked their seidels together and the Assessor looked at the flowing Danube for a while, and then, reaching into his coat, he took a billfold out and switched to a happier theme. He placed the billfold on the table, carefully drew from it a newspaper clipping, unfolded it, and handed it to the Gauleiter. "Appeared this morning," he said, leaning close to enjoy the reading of his latest poem once again, together with the Gauleiter.

The lips of the Gauleiter formed the words silently. "Also, I must say, really—no, I mean it—it's wonderful. I can't understand how you do it," he remarked reverently and handed the poem back.

"It's not easy!" said the poet.

"I can believe that," said the animal with the voice. "I have had trouble with words all my life."

"Well, I must confess nothing makes me happier than

when I am through with one of my poems. I fold it up, stick it in an envelope, I lick the envelope and walk to the mailbox and start it on its way to the editor in Nuremberg."

"You are proud then, yes, Herr Assessor?"

"Yes, proud, and greatly relieved, Herr Gauleiter. For example, I have sat up several nights thinking of this one. Once I begin to think of it, I can't let it go—you know, it follows me around the moment I begin to think of it, like a dog that you are afraid will eventually bite you."

The Gauleiter pointed at the poem. "But this," he said, "but this is just as if you had written it down in a minute."

"That is just it—it's free, it's good. If it seems hard or tight, it isn't any good at all. You want to know how it is?" he asked, moving closer. "It's as if you were constipated. For days you feel a stone in here, and nothing happens. You drag yourself around, you have cramps in your intestines, and you are too upset to sleep. And then suddenly it loosens up and it flows, like beautiful music, easy and free."

The Gauleiter nodded with understanding. "I follow you exactly," he said. "Explain to me—how do you think of the words?"

The poet put a finger to the side of his nose. "First of all there is the mood. The mood is as necessary as the words. I poet best when I march at the head of my platoon, or when I see marchers passing before me. That always inspires me, and, of course, our flag most of all. The rhythm helps, the feeling that goes through you. I also get into the mood on trains, the passing telegraph poles, the clatter of the wheels as they go over the rail joints. There is rhythm again—that is good. I have written some of my best poems on trains."

"I mean, how do you find the words?" said the Gauleiter.

"I am coming to that in just a minute. That's the most important part of the whole thing."

"Excuse me," said the Gauleiter and ordered another seidel for himself.

"For example, I can poet beautifully in this garden."

"But nothing moves here," interrupted the Gauleiter.

"Of course it moves; the Danube there drags it out of me. For example, this poem you have just read grew in this garden. You would never think it—the first inspiration, Herr Gauleiter, came from that red and white striped awning there, the one that hangs over the entrance. Do you see that awning over there?"

"Yes," said the Gauleiter, "but there's nothing about an awning in this poem here."

"Oh, yes, there is," said the poet. Gritting his teeth, he leaned down from his ivory tower to explain the secret alchemy of his art to the Dummkopf Stolz. "When you look at the awning, Herr Gauleiter, the white and red stripes—what does that remind you of?"

"An awning," said the Gauleiter.

"More," said the poet, "much more, Herr Gauleiter. It is made of canvas, and keeps the sun and rain out and therefore it suggests a tent, and the white and red stripes —what do they suggest?" There was no reaction. "Well, I will tell you what they made me think of—they suggested the American flag to me." The poet took a piece of paper from his pocket and wrote on it the German word for tent, which is Zelt. "Now, what does the American flag remind us of?" he asked, and when he encountered silence again he answered himself, "It reminds us of Roosevelt, whose true name is Rosenfeld."

"Remarkable," said the Gauleiter, shifting his body; he became very interested.

The poet wrote "Rosenfeld" under "Zelt." "Now," he said, and pointed at the first two lines of the poem, "see what we have there." The Gauleiter read:

> In his striped and star-spangled Zelt
> Sits one whose name is Rosenfeld.

"Colossal and so simple!" exclaimed the animal with the voice. He banged on the table with his fist. "Go on."

"All right—now we go on. Besides stripes the American flag is decorated with stars. Now, what do stars remind you of, Herr Gauleiter?"

"Don't tell me—I know," said the Gauleiter, eagerly. "The Jews."

"Right," screamed the poet. "And what do the Jews remind us of?"

"Money," yelled the Gauleiter.

"Yes, yes, very good, excellent, perfect! And something else they remind us of—think awhile."

The Gauleiter's eyes dimmed and the poet came to his rescue. "Mo—" he said, "Mor— Morgen—" The Gauleiter looked at him hopelessly. "What do you see on the leaves of trees and on the grass in the morning?"

"Dew, Thau," said the Gauleiter as he saw the light. "Morgenthau," he said. "Ah, now we have it."

The poet had written the German word for money, which is Geld, on the paper. He observed that it rhymes with Welt, world. "Now," he said, "let's read the whole poem—let's read it again from the start."

> *In his striped and star-spangled Zelt*
> *Sits one whose name is Rosenfeld.*
> *The Jews from all over the Welt*
> *Run to the Zelt and Rosenfeld,*
> *Where Morgenthau the Jewish Geld*
> *With his filthy fingers zählt.*

"Got twenty-five marks for it. I must say it's not one of my best; the word zählt—to count—doesn't exactly rhyme with Geld, but you can't be too particular, and even our great Goethe has taken similar liberties."

"I call it wunderbar. It's remarkable, Herr Assessor. I wish I had a gift like yours," said the animal with the voice, and called for Frau Saltner to pay his bill.

On the way to the bridge they stopped at a tobacco shop owned by a Party member. The Gauleiter slowly and with great care selected two cheap cigars and cut the ends off. He lit one and put the other in his pocket, and after a hundred feet on the upgrade of the bridge, he asked, "What are you going to write about next?"

The Assessor walked in back of him—the sidewalk was only wide enough for one person—and he answered loudly, "I shall write something about an Island in the Danube, radishes—and three gypsies."

The Gauleiter stopped and looked at the Island. "If they lived in a back street we could get at them easier, or out in the woods, or in Reinhausen. You wouldn't have

to bother with poetry or licenses. But down there everyone can see them. All day long their pump goes, the two
old crows fly up and down, and when that pump stands
still, people will ask what has happened to them. It's like
a body with a heart beating, and when the heart stands
still people know somebody's died."

The Assessor stopped alongside the Gauleiter, who
leaned over the stone banister, blew cigar smoke into the
wind, and looked down. The pig lay in the mud on the
shore of the Island, old Anton and the young girl carried
the watering cans alongside rows of young radish plants,
and the two old sisters sailed up and down on the pump.

The poet opened his mouth. "Permit me to say that
you yourself are a poet, Herr Gauleiter—the lord and
ladies of radish island, the two old crows, the heart stands
still—your words are not bad. My respects." They came
to the bridgetower and, in the cool shadow of the fortifi-
cations that form its base, the friends shook hands. The
Gauleiter went back to his dry goods shop, and the Assessor to his new office.

In a week of expert chicanery, and with the closest
co-operation of the police, the Bureau of Markets, and
the Bureau of Licenses, the Assessor had attained his objective. He was on duty at the tower on Sunday morning
in his capacity as air-raid warden, and he trained his binoculars on the Island. He was eager to see what they would
do now that he had made the sale of radishes at the beer
garden impossible. He looked, and it became clear that
all his work had been for nothing. Happy as birds—as if
there was no authority in this world that concerned them,
as if there was no such thing as a Bureau of Licenses—the

people on the Island carried the radishes down to the
boat. Anton helped his sisters and the young girl into it
and pushed out into the river. They crossed the Strudel,
but when they came to land, they did not go their usual
way. They went up through the Street of Beautiful Opportunity and crossed the small park that separated the
Bishop's residence from the cathedral, and they approached it just as the bells of the cathedral began to ring
High Mass.

The Assessor got the Gauleiter on the telephone. "The
gypsies have carried their hampers up through the city,
up the steps of the cathedral." The poet used the deroga-
tory Bavarian term for priests, which is Pfaffen. He said
that two Pfaffen had come out of the church and smiled
at them and showed them where to place their radish
baskets. "They've got two new Saints at the portal of the
cathedral," said the poet. "They sit among the Gothic
statuary—the same false and holy faces, their eyes downcast, their lips pointed like the rear ends of plucked
ducks, Saint Martha and Saint Anna—and the Pfaffen
hold their fat hands over them in protection."

"For years they have been the Bishop's pets," said the
Gauleiter. "Their bones would be rotting long ago but
for that. It's the Bishop who told them to sell the radishes in front of the cathedral. They have it thick behind
the ears, they and the Pfaffen."

The Gauleiter said he would see what could be done.
He dressed in a hurry in civilian clothes and walked up
toward the cathedral.

Half an hour later the animal with the voice appeared
below, in the cathedral square. He was the size of a

thimble and the poet brought him close with his binoculars. The Gauleiter climbed the steps of the cathedral, stopped before the Saints, looked at the radish hampers, and then walked into the cathedral. He remained inside the church for the length of the service and came out with the crowd, stopping again to watch the sale of the radishes. The two hampers emptied themselves almost as fast as if they had been turned upside down. The animal with the voice tried to remember all the people who bought radishes. He walked down to the bridge and over the Danube into the beer garden.

"Himmel—Herrgott Sakrament!" he said. "It beats anything I have experienced in my life—it makes me the laughing stock of Regensburg." He called Frau Saltner and ordered his food. "It almost takes my appetite away," he observed, holding the menu in his hand. He continued wearily, "I have never felt like this about anything. Who do they think they are! What do they permit themselves! The filthy beggars! The gypsies! The nose-pickers!"

"Who stops us from taking those miserable crows by their dirty necks and throwing the Communist swine into a concentration camp!" said the poet.

"The Bishop," said the Gauleiter. "It's difficult to eat cherries with that Pfaff. I wish you had arranged something different."

"The Bishop sleeps too well these days," said the poet. "His glaziers' bill has gotten low. There hasn't been a parade for a long time, no public expression of disgust, like the time when not a window on two sides of his palace was left whole."

"Yes," said the Gauleiter, "write something about that,

why don't you? Not about Rosenfeld or Morgenthau, Herr Poet. Write about the Bishop, about the Pfaff, over there across the river. You see that big building with the two golden crosses on it across the river—there, Herr Assessor—the tall building with the two spires, which you can see twenty miles away in any direction? What does it remind you of, Herr Poet?" The poet was quiet. "It reminds me of a cathedral—and a Bishop—and of the fact that you have made a Dummkopf out of me, Herr Assessor!" The Gauleiter stopped to look at the food which Frau Saltner had placed before him. He took knife and fork, and for several minutes he labored efficiently in the oval-shaped, heavy porcelain dish, stabbing, cutting, swishing sauce up the sides, and soaking it up with pieces of dumpling. While his mouth was still full, so that he could hardly say Pfaff, and only a dry piece of dumpling was left in a corner, he pushed the dish away, and mumbled, "—that Goddamned Pfaff. I can't eat any more. Take it away, Frau Saltner. My appetite is gone." His chair grated in the sand as he turned to call after Frau Saltner, who had taken his rejected dish away—he wanted to order an additional beer. As he looked after her, he saw old Anton, his two sisters, and Leni come into the beer garden. They sat down at the only free table, which was close to that of the Gauleiter.

"If I wasn't here myself I wouldn't believe it," he said with a dry angry voice. "There they are, in the flesh— Saint Anna, Saint Martha, and the fine brother." He turned away from the table. "Tell me what they are doing," he said to the Assessor.

The poet looked at them and said. "Just now the old

man is slicing the radishes, and Frau Saltner has brought them each a glass of beer."

"I have to wait half an hour before I get any attention here, but the lord and ladies of radish island, the Bishop's pets, they get attention immediately after they sit down. You know, there is a lot wrong here."

In the center of each of the tables in the beer garden Zur Blauen Donau stood a miniature chromium pole flying a small flag on which the emblem of the Party appeared. The Gauleiter watched the flag on his table for a while and played with the cord to which it was attached. He decided to move his chair. He looked across to the table on which the people of the Island sat, particularly to find out if there, too, was one of the flags. He saw the flag, and after looking across several times after that, he abruptly got up, walked over, lifted his hat, and picked up the flag.

"Excuse me," he said, "I thought it might annoy you, Herr Fischer."

The old man looked at him steadily and said, "Thank you."

The Gauleiter set the flag down at the table beside his own, straightened up and held his sides, rocking with made laughter. " 'Thank you,' he says. Did you hear that?" he yelled. He pointed at the table. "He said 'thank you.' Please, Herr Fischer, don't mention it. You have a fine voice, Herr Fischer," he continued, and, addressing himself to the audience, he said, "Have you ever heard him sing? The Herr Fischer has a fine voice." Nobody looked at the Gauleiter. They all sat still. The men seemed more interested in their beer and the women in their hands. "Herr Kapellmeister, you wouldn't know the melody of the 'Internationale'—to play for Herr Fischer? Sing it for us, Herr Fischer. Why don't you? What did you say, Herr Fischer?" Old Anton had said nothing; he looked at the animal with the voice. "He says his throat is sore," said the Gauleiter, speaking on behalf of the old man. "Please, sing something for us, a Wiegenlied, or why not our anthem?" The Gauleiter gave a performance for the beer garden. As if the old man had spoken again, Stolz turned his ear down toward him and made believe he listened; he held up his hands, asking for silence; he addressed the people; he apologized.

"Herr Fischer says he can't sing, he's very sorry. He doesn't know the words of our anthem. Oh, your throat isn't sore. I stood beside you in the cathedral, Herr Fischer, when you sang the Te Deum this morning louder than all the Pfaffen put together, and in Latin. What a pity you can't remember our anthem. It's written in simple words, German words—I'll give you the first words Herr Fischer. They are: 'Die Fahne hoch.' "

"That's not my anthem," said the old man quietly, and got up. "I'll sing an anthem, an old one, when your monkey chatter stops, when something better comes along than you."

"Anton, Anton," said the sisters and pulled on his sleeves.

"Oh, let him talk, we all want to hear what he has to say," said the Gauleiter.

Somebody in the crowd shouted, "Anton, don't be a fool. Keep your mouth shut. For God's sake, sit down, Anton!"

Anton spoke: "You keep your mouths shut, you stay as you are. Don't lift a hand to come to my aid, not a whisper of agreement, not a nod in my direction—God help any one of you who does. Stay as you are, look down into your mugs or they'll write your name down and your thin beer will come out of you mixed with your blood.

"Tremble with fear—it's your old illness. You're the untouchables of Europe, you remain uncomplaining, while they do with you as they wish—with your life, your children, and your property. They've always had their hands in your pockets and now that the pockets are empty, they lay hands on your nakedness, they feel your haunches like butchers, to see how much more in labor and in sweat is in you, and when that is taken, you'll be nice corpses with obedient faces. Cattle live and die better.

"You have forgotten to complain—oh, they let you complain. They are happy when you denounce your neighbor, they profit when friend distrusts friend, when you become afraid to look into your children's faces. But go and complain about men like these two here that have ridden you into misery, cry out about the crimes they have committed against you, laugh at the idiots' blabber they declare the law of the land, and they will smash your faces with shovels and trample you into silence. You have always stood before them in your sweaty shirts, the obedient, and with patience, waiting in line, mute and fawning for the approval of the least of them. And they, they have only changed their uniform—once it was blue, now it's brown, and when this is over it will be yellow or gray or blue again."

"He's a philosopher, that one," said the poet—he had taken notes.

The sand crunched. Anton came toward the table. "Look up, friends. They're not dangerous when you get close to them." He walked to the Gauleiter, reached inside his collar with one hand, took the glasses off his face, and then smacked him left and right until his hand hurt and tears ran down his face. He pushed him back into his seat and walked quietly out of the garden.

The Gauleiter almost fell off his chair. He sat back like a sack, pale, his arms hanging down. The animal with the voice seemed to suffer from a stroke—he was purple and he choked. The Assessor was under the table looking for the Gauleiter's glasses.

A team of percherons thundered through the passage into the beer garden, dragging a wagon stacked high with barrels, and after it had turned toward the shed where the beer was served, Joseph Lintl, the Bishop of Regensburg, appeared in the passage, accompanied by his small gray dog. He propelled himself with a rolled-up umbrella, and, on account of the heat, his hat was attached with a clip to his cassock. He sat down at the table which had been vacated by the Island's people; he mopped his head and face, ordered his food, and lit a cigar.

The Gauleiter and the poet left, and the garden still remained quiet. A flock of sparrows that lived off the beer garden, the quarrelsome, gray-brown, trashy bird people, became audible.

They had spent a while with a few chickens that were kept in a wire cage at the end of the establishment. The loops in the wire were just large enough, and conveniently rounded, for the sparrows to get through. They had stolen the corn away from in front of the beaks of the chickens, and they had hopped back through the wire into several muddy puddles that were left from rainfall of the night before. In these they bathed noisily, splashing and ruffling their plumage.

Like balls of old newspaper, thrown away, they advanced in clumsy hopping and jerky flight toward the fence, passed between the pickets out onto a strip of grass and the sunlight, and there they argued until one among them, with shrill piping, signaled the approach of an enemy. With shifty, watchful eyes and quick turns of the head they watched the passing cat and at the same time kept an eye on the Bishop who was about to break a roll in half. They hopped back through the pickets, to the rungs of chairs that stood near the Bishop's table, and when he brushed the crumbs off, the birds fell over themselves again, fluttered and fought and argued with their unmusical, abominable voices that go: "Tel tel—shill shell seelb, chk chk, peep peep."

"How nice and quiet it is here today," the Bishop said to Frau Saltner. He had a theory that before drinking beer when one is hot, a swallow of Schnaps should be taken. He poured the contents of a short heavy glass of liquor down his throat.

"Yes, it's very quiet here today, your Grace," said Frau Saltner.

The Bishop took a deep draught of beer and looked around. A plate of short roasted sausages arrived, and the Bishop asked where Herr Fischer was.

"Old Anton?" said Frau Saltner, as if she tried very

hard to remember someone whose name is lost. "He isn't here any more." It was a phrase that everyone in Regensburg understood.

"Oh," said the Bishop. A cold wind blew from the Danube, and one by one the tables in the beer garden emptied.

CHAPTER
6

FRAU SALTNER rendered the guests of the Blue Danube the worst service of a long career, after the incident in the beer garden. Only after people waved napkins, called for her several times, and knocked with their knives on the sides of their steins, did she interrupt herself. She rushed beer and goulashes, dumplings, and noodles to the customers as quickly as she could, so she could get back as fast as possible to describing old Anton's attack on the Gauleiter. She stood under the tree where it happened. "Here sat the Gauleiter," she started off. "Right next to him, on this chair, was the Assessor, and over there sat Herr Fischer with his two sisters and the girl." Besides the regular visitors to the beer garden, people poured in off the street, not to eat or drink, but to listen to Frau Saltner's recital. She gave better voice and words to Anton's speech than he had. She stood as a living Statue of Liberty in the center of the beer garden, and those who listened to her kept their mouths open in astonishment and rapture, their heads were held sideways to hear her better, and since they were afraid to nod with approval or to smile, they looked instead as if they were very hungry. Toward the end of the story, Frau Saltner became vehement; she advanced on the group of her listeners, suddenly reached inside of the collar of the man closest to her, exactly as old Anton had done, and swished her hand right and left before his face, showing how the Gauleiter had been slapped.

If there was an official among those listening or an individual of whom she was not altogether sure, then she added a few words to the recital; she changed her tune then, and said at the end, "It surprised me terribly when I heard the old fool talk that way. You never know what people think. He came here for years, always quiet, always orderly, never opened his mouth, and then to talk like that to a Gauleiter."

It was never printed or broadcast in Regensburg, but the story got outside the garden and eventually, when one saw two Regensburgers standing together on the Danube bridge or the stone quay, in a beer garden or on a side street, and one took hold of the other by the collar and sent his hand flying through the air in front of his face, then every child and idiot knew what they were talking about. The gesture became as common as the Party salute. Since everyone added his own grievances to it, the speech as told a week after it was delivered by old Anton had grown until the average version ran for fifteen minutes.

The recitals in the beer garden stopped only when the animal with the voice or Assessor Unruh appeared. They sat again at their accustomed table and waited for food and drink, but no matter how long it took, the Gauleiter did not complain about the service, he never tapped with the knife at the side of his seidel or announced his hunger and thirst in any of the usual fashions—he waited patiently until she came to his table and then he did not look at Frau Saltner; he gave his order, and she in turn made believe that it was not he when she brought his food and drink. On one of the first days after the trouble, the poet took a clipping of the incident out of his billfold, and spread it before the Gauleiter. It appeared under the title "The Lord of Radish Island" in the *Stürmer*. But Herr Stolz pushed it away; he was grateful that it had not been picked up by the *Regensburger Anzeiger*.

"I promise you, Herr Gauleiter," said the Assessor, "that he will not escape. He is the only German who doesn't legally exist; he is lost the moment the first policeman asks him for his papers. Besides, I promise you he'll come back. He has nothing in the world to live for but the Island, the old crows, and his niece. I promise you, he will come back. He must come back, he knows that they need him, they will starve to death without him. Who is going to row them through the Strudel? They stood there on the quay the day it happened and waited. A peasant from Reinhausen rowed them across, and then the peasant had to go home and he took his boat with him, and since then they stand there at the waterline, and stupidly look at the river and across at their boat, and they wonder how they will get over the river. They can't get through the Strudel—they'll drown. They have a whole week to think, until Sunday comes. There will be no radishes for sale at the beer garden, or at the cathedral. We have them, I promise you that, exactly where we want them, Herr Gauleiter. What good is the Bishop and the cathedral if you can't row the radishes through the Strudel?"

"How do you know all this?" wearily inquired the animal with the voice.

"I have the Island before me all the time. I see it from my office, and especially well from my tower, Herr Gauleiter. I have nothing to do up on that tower. I stay there because I am an air-raid warden and ordered to do so, but you and I know that it is a waste of time. The Government has said that no enemy plane will ever get this far. Since I have nothing else to do up there, I watch. I'll keep my eyes on them. Closely measured, it's three hundred and fifty yards from the tower to the furthest point of the Island, and through my telescopic sight I can see a fly on the nose of either of the old crows. Nothing escapes me. When I am not there my relief men are. The Island is watched twenty-four hours a day. Herr Gauleiter, he will come back—he must come back. The moment he comes back, you shall know it; you, Herr Gauleiter, shall be the first to know. You shall have the personal satisfaction and the pleasure of dealing with him."

The Gauleiter brought both fists down on the table. "Unruh, I can't sleep since that happened. I'm not the same any more. On the street it's as if I was walking in front of myself—I have to push myself ahead of myself through the city across the bridge into this garden, and sit here and know they're all laughing at me. We have to do something."

"He will come back," said the poet. "Don't worry, he will come back."

The next day the Gauleiter, dressed in a business suit, walked up along the stone quay. He carried the oars to his boat and steered it toward the Island. He allowed it to drift past, and, coming out of the Strudel, he turned into the calm waters at the far end of the Island. He got out. Crawling over two large stones, he made his boat fast to the stump of a willow tree, and, remembering that he was unarmed, he reached down into the boat and took his heavy cane along. He hung it over his arm and advanced along the shore. He walked slowly, carefully examining the loamy earth for footprints. He stood still awhile and listened. There was the sound of the river. The hinge of the old pump yammered in intervals of half seconds. The pig grunted somewhere close by. He saw it up ahead surrounded by daisies. He found its back caked with dry mud, the belly wet; it was happily uprooting slime. The animal with the voice turned and walked toward the house. One of the old crows was on the pump, along with the young girl. The girl was very beautiful. The Gauleiter walked carefully along the path. He looked at the pump several times, and when he came to it, he stopped beside it. He stood absolutely, solidly still, not knowing that he did so, his provocative and obscene face uplifted, his eyes following the falling and rising figure above him. He was glued to her ankles, he stared for an endless while at the girl's smooth, white, supple knees and watched the variations of shadow and light which her swinging skirts played on her limbs; enjoyed the sinewy, light balance of her body; saw her rising on the palms of her bare feet. His wide nostrils drank in the moist, warm and heavy air, the perfume of her person, of herbs and sunshine, that passed him as she sank. He made immediate room for her in his affections. He took a close look at her hips and shoulders as she came down the ladder—he had placed himself so that she had to brush by him to get to the house. In two steps she was before him, her firm bosom fell and rose, she wiped the hair from her forehead with the back of her hand, and her frank blue eyes looked at him with feminine inquiry. He was scared by the face of the old crow who followed after her. He stepped back, smelled hay and wildflowers, and thought of himself as a donkey—he had not taken his hat off as she passed, had said no word; he had merely taken the cigar out of his mouth after she was past him. When she was fifty feet from him, he regretted that he had not shown himself more the man of the world: several gallant things that he might have said came to his mind. He regretted when she was a hundred feet away that he had not shown himself the man of absolute authority, with power over life and death. He rowed back and went to his house, where he drew the velure curtains and lay down to rest on the couch in his living room. He thought of the Island. He imagined a scene in which he took the girl of the pump into the bushes. He remembered a scene with the maid he had inherited, together with the house and the business, from Emanuel Kempinski and Sons. She was a Catholic peasant girl. Long ago, a while after he had taken office, when he still was a Gruppenführer, he had surprised her in his room as she was making his bed. "Confess to me," he had shouted at her, "that you had relations with the old Jew who owned this house and with his sons."

She had begged him on her knees. "I swear to God," she had cried, "I swear by my mother, by the dear Virgin Mary, I haven't. I've never had anything to do with any man."

"We shall see," he had said, as he pressed her down

into his bed with one hand, and held her mouth closed
with the other. That had been long ago, and the good
girl had not been lying and was taken care of. She became
one of the first properly unwed mothers—he had seen to
that. All the papers were in order, the strapping boy was
now a member of the Youth Movement and a credit to
his mother. That was one way of doing it. Nothing to
stop him—the peasant girl was plain, with a blubbery
pigface and eyebrows like two black caterpillars, and there
was little one could feel about her. She had cried a few
days and gone back to Reinhausen, and when it was all
over, she had returned to work in the Gauleiter's house
and was still there, and a very satisfactory servant. The
Gauleiter had forgotten almost completely about the incident until the girl of the pump had brought it back to
his memory. He allowed the story to pass through his
mind; he found it still exciting.

The animal with the voice got up from his afternoon
rest. He sat on the edge of the couch for a while and
yawned and scratched himself; he got up, pulled back the
curtains and arranged his clothes. A while after, he went
out. He walked toward the stone bridge. Half-way across,
he stopped and leaned on the balustrade and looked
down at the Island. The girl was carrying the heavy watering can; in the center of a row of radish plants she put it
down, straightened up, pulled her lovely shoulders back,
and, using the familiar gesture, reached up and brushed
the hair out of her eyes with the back of her hand. Then
she continued with her work. He waited until she had
finished a second row, and then he lit a cigar. He thought
that she was working too hard; he felt sorry for her.

Beauty always begets sympathy and respect. He decided that with her he would proceed in a new and different fashion. With pleasure for both parties, he hoped. He flicked his match away and watched it fall down into the Strudel. This time he would do it with tenderness, with elegance, take time and trouble. It would be romantic, with perhaps a gift from the dry goods establishment even. After a while he tore himself away from the small paradise in the river Danube and, continuing across the bridge, he lifted his legs with more ease; he swung his cane; he even returned the greeting of a passing Under-expeditor of the post office of Stadt am Hof with much more joviality than was due that individual; and he was humming a pleasant tune as he stopped at the end of the bridge and looked into the display window of a Wurst-geschäft. The Gauleiter went in to make his daily purchase, and when the saleswoman who weighed his four slices of sausage asked him, "Ja wie gehts denn, Herr Gauleiter?" he answered louder than usual; he said: "Mir gehts wunderbar!" Then he walked to the beer garden.

"Don't bother getting up," he said to the waiting Assessor Unruh. He hung his hat and cane on a tree, sat down and put his arm on the bloodbrother's shoulder. "Do you know," he asked, "anything about love—I mean, how to write about love?"

"But, certainly, Herr Gauleiter," said the poet. "What kind of a poet is a poet who doesn't know how to write about love, particularly, what kind of a German poet? The German language is richer in the words of love than any other. We have more love songs and poems than any nation on earth."

The Gauleiter said, "Why don't you write something about a girl like the Lorelei—combs her golden hair—sits on a rock in the Strudel?"

The poet looked out at the Danube. "I don't know who the lady is," he said, "but allow me to remark that 'Strudel' is an unfortunate word. The only other words it rhymes with are noodle and poodle, and in love one can't be funny. You will never attain your objective if you invoke laughter. In that game the first rule is absolute seriousness. It's like religion, or thinking about the Führer."

The Gauleiter thanked him for the advice. He took a thick wallet from his pocket and placed an envelope on the table which he took from among other papers. The poet hoped to see a clipping of his work, but the Gauleiter opened the envelope and produced two thin slices of salami and two of liverwurst. He picked up a slice of salami and held it under the poet's nose. "Wunderbar," said the poet. "Wunderbar is right," said the Gauleiter and placed the four slices of sausage on his plate, elaborating therewith a cold plate which consisted of a thin cut of ham, another of cold pork, a quarter of a hardboiled egg, and a ladle of potato salad. The poet, who could not afford to eat out and only came for beer, watched him eat and then spilled the words of love on the table before them—he said it was the easiest form of poetry.

I, you, Danube, blue, your hand, golden band,
sunset, duty, war, far away, sad and gay,
girl, moonlight, kiss, and bended knee,
Pfaffen, blood, Fatherland, the Führer, you and me.

"Blonde?" asked the Assessor.

The Gauleiter was removing the skin of the second slice of sausage carefully. "I think so," he said, "but I'll have to go and look at her once more. I'm not certain."

The cold plate was taken away, and the second course came, a goulash with sauerkraut and two potato dumplings. It is considered wrong in Regensburg to cut a dumpling with a knife—the saying goes that one cuts the cook's heart that way. The Gauleiter at times was a very sentimental man. He held the dumplings down with the knife, one at a time, rubbed them in sauce, and tore them to pieces with the prongs of the fork, which is the alternative to cutting them. "Yes, I think she is blonde," he said, when he noticed that the Assessor had rhymed blonde with Mond, the German word for moon.

On one of the four hundred square blocks of granite that form the sidewalk on the stone bridge, they stopped on the way back from the beer garden, and swearing him to absolute silence, the Gauleiter confided his attachment to the girl on the pump. "I congratulate you, but we shall have to change it," said the Assessor. "The poem, I mean. She's light brown, I know; I look at her every day." The Gauleiter followed him all the way to the tower, where the Assessor handed him the binoculars. "Look," he said, and pointed below, "light brown." He himself looked through the telescopic sight of his gun. "In the morning, when the sun is low, it looks sometimes like pure gold, and also when the sun sets. The rest of the time it's light brown. But anyway, I congratulate you," said the Assessor. "You have an eye for beauty. That changes the picture as far as old Anton is concerned. For a certain favor granted you may allow the old man to come back. You can be generous, make it last a few weeks, until the first quarrel, and then we have two birds with one stone," said the Assessor.

The reflection of sunlight shone up from the river into the bells of the Glockenspiel. It placed weaving light patterns on the metal and on the ancient woodwork overhead. The clock's mechanism below them began to work. A whirring sound started the wheels going, wires pulled, dry beams groaned and the tower shook, and on the outside the figure of a man with an arrow passed, announcing the half hour. A hammer overhead lifted, fell on one of the smaller bells, lifted again and fell once more, and then the concert of noises stopped. The Gauleiter took his hands from his ears. "I am used to it. I hold mine only when it strikes the full hour," said the Assessor. "When I have the morning watch I go below at ten and at eleven, and at quarter to twelve. It's enough to drive you mad. You can hold your ears, but the sound comes in anyway. It comes through your nose and through the bones. I find that opening your mouth helps somewhat; that's what artillery men do when they fire their guns."

The structure stopped vibrating, and the birds that had flown away at the beginning of the whirring of the wheels came back to the tower. The Assessor said that he would polish the poem a little and leave it at the Gauleiter's house as he went home. He shook hands with Herr Stolz and saluted. He walked the first few rough steps that led to the scaffolding below, holding the Gauleiter's arm and letting him down carefully as if he were a precious weight in a bag. Then, before he said his final good-night, on the third platform beneath the clock mechanism, he took courage, blocked the Gauleiter's way, and said, "I would be most respectfully grateful if, at the next meeting of the Magistrates, it could be brought to the notice of that body that Assessor Nebenzahl has been in the shoes of an Oberassessor for a good while now, and a promotion to that position would be—"

"Yes, yes," said the Gauleiter, "I have the ear of the Herr Burgomaster; I shall see what can be done. As in love, everything lies in correct timing, Herr Assessor. I shall put a word in for you at the right moment."

"Thank you, Herr Gauleiter," said the Assessor, and ran back up to his post.

After a night filled with wondrous images, the Gauleiter rowed over to the Island again. His boat bobbed through the Strudel and drifted into calm water. He threw the chain gaily over the stump of the willow tree, and with newfound agility he jumped on land and walked up to the house. With crossed arms, like a drill sergeant surveying the exercises of a recruit, he stopped and stood at the side of the pump again, blowing cigar smoke into the air. His eyes followed her up and down. He thought that she was more beautiful even than the day before, but he could not speak. She looked at him, and the Gauleiter felt weak. The bitter juices dripped down his insides. The dreadful compulsion of love, stronger even than the Party, took hold of him; he joined a lockstep more close and inevitable than that of any prison. He tried to escape for a while by walking away and lighting another of his bad cigars, but as he looked back, he was in aching chains again. He walked at last toward the house in which they lived. After all, he had come on a tour of inspection. He examined the house thoroughly, outside and in; he looked into the kitchen, and into the room where the old sisters slept. He walked up a stairway, to a low place under the roof where the girl seemed to live. He hung his cane on the rafters and opened a drawer. He noticed small articles of linen, a partly done embroidery, the small belongings of a young girl, a pair of gloves, white and hand-knitted, a forget-me-not blue medallion of the Virgin, a paper calendar with a picture of the Grotto of Altötting, a small blue pillow, a prayerbook of blue velvet. Blue seemed to be her favorite color; her eyes were like the blue of corn-flowers. He also found a child's toy parasol and an album with dried field flowers. He unpacked, searched, came to another place where a shirt hung, and he pressed it to his face. It smelled of young woman, of the attic. He held the shirt away from himself so that it opened and he could see how it hung—whether, in unfolding, it would reveal the outline of her form. He put it away and sat down on the bed; for a while he busied himself opening and closing the toy umbrella. Then he heard her voice. He looked out of the window and saw her below, warm and young, her cheeks burning; her bosom rose higher than usual, and again she wiped hair from her forehead with the back of her hand. Saint Martha and Saint Anna waited below. They did not know what he wanted, but they sensed, and when he came down they looked at him as stone-eyed as the saints at the portals of the church. "Do what you have to do, Gauleiter, and be off," they said. "You've seen our house and you've had your look

at the Island. Old Anton isn't here, or the yard would be in order and the dead branches picked up."

"I am as lenient as I can be," he said. "It could be worse for you, much worse. I have my duty to perform."

Fire burned in back of their eyes. "Sleep after your meals, Gauleiter, and leave decent people alone. You'll find nothing here but trouble."

He became resentful that he was not liked, and he turned and said quietly to the girl: "If you know where he is, tell him to come back. No harm will come to him."

She listened and said nothing. He was rooted again to where he stood. She leaned against the pump, one arm up, the other hanging loosely at her side, the feet together. She was a statue holding an invisible urn on her right shoulder; she looked at him and he ached as he looked at her, and then he woke up, moved his eyes, and turned and left. "Tell Anton Fischer he can come back if he wants to. Nothing will happen to him," he said to the sisters over his shoulder.

The poem was very satisfactory, the sun shone the next morning, and the Gauleiter got up, called for the maid, and sent his uniform into the kitchen to have it pressed and gave her the boots and belt to shine. He went to his shop in his underwear and rummaged in various drawers until he found a red silk kerchief and a pair of white gloves of prewar quality, thin and bedded in a long box, gloves such as were sold to the parents of young girls for their first communion. He wrapped the lot in pink tissue, added a small bottle of Parisian perfume, and the poem. He came out of his house in full regalia, his belt as well as his boots shone, and he wore gloves. He walked to his boat, rowed across the Danube, and as usual he let the boat drift to the Island where he repeated his inspection. He loitered outside the kitchen, examined the windows, entered the house, and walked up to the low room, stood alone beside Leni's bed, and put the package on her pillow. The old crows waited for him again, each one with a cane in her right hand, and the girl was beside them until he came out of the house. They saw that he was without the package. Then she ran upstairs and brought it down. She placed it on the table, took off the ribbon, opened the box, took out the handkerchief, the gloves, slowly opened the letter, and read it aloud. At the end, she looked at him as if he had come from another world, she looked at the old sisters, and the three began to laugh until their sides hurt them. Saint Martha leaned on the pump, Saint Anna sat down on the stoop of the house—it was long, loud laughter. They wheezed like a blacksmith's bellows as they tried to get air. Leni carefully packed the things together and put everything back in the box. She ran after the Gauleiter, who was in his boat. She swept her skirts high, waded out until the water was above her knees, and carefully placed the package on the back seat of the boat. She looked at him again with inquiry in her blue eyes, and without malice—she seemed capable only of love—said "Thank you." The laughter still came to him over the waves. While he rowed, he looked up at the tower and saw the binoculars trained on him. He fastened his boat, snapped the padlock, and walked home to his wife.

CHAPTER

7

THEY had broken the windows of the Bishop's palace
at night, and written obscenities on its walls. They
kept up caterwauling and name calling as long as he was
out of sight, but when he appeared they put their hands
into their pockets, lit cigarettes, and shoved off. Even the
buffoons of the Party and the worst ruffians became sheep-
eyed. When the Bishop of Regensburg walked through
the town, the most glittering uniforms, the shiniest boots
went off the sidewalk.

In his immense form, he represented the good things
of Heaven and of earth. His voice was clearly audible in
the last recesses of his cathedral, and when he walked, the
people whose faces turned to him, to those who looked
into his eyes, he gave of his strength, he was the last
anchor, the only vessel of decency, their only hope. As his
portly form advanced at a slow pace, the immense face
shone, his umbrella swung at his side; and the gray little
dog with his rough coat, his red tongue hanging out, his
red eyes blinking, looked like the devil, cowed and sub-
servient, with his tail cut off, running in back of the
Bishop. He appeared daily in the streets of Regensburg,
a fortress of faith.

The Bishop walked along the quay and looked at
the rowboats which shifted back and forth in the currents
of the Danube. They were attached to iron rings along

the stones. He did not see a single boat that would have supported him.

Saint Anna and Saint Martha were sailing up and down on the pump across on the Island. He waved at them with his umbrella, and they waved back. Leni was carrying water to the plants. The Bishop made one of his rare gestures of futility, holding both arms out and shrugging his shoulders, and then he walked across the bridge to the beer garden where he sat down, drank a small Kirsch, and followed it with a glass of beer. He fed the birds, and Frau Saltner brought his dog a bone. He listened again to the story of old Anton, told without gestures. He told her that he would like to go to the Island but did not know how to get there. After some thought, and looking at the river and the Island, Frau Saltner said that unless he swam there was only one way—the boat that could take him was a barge, an old boat which floated down river every day with provisions from Regensburg for the village of Donaustauf and for the keepers of the Walhalla, and was pulled back to Regensburg by two horses. To get that man to stop at the Island, and then continue with him down to the Walhalla, was the only way for the Bishop to see his parishioners. The Bishop asked Frau Saltner to arrange passage on the barge for him.

The boatman made a comfortable seat for the Bishop, and the barge shot through the fifth arch of the Danube and headed for the Island. The sun was low as he arrived; it still warmed the Bishop's broad back. It glowed in the large cakes of ice on the barge and placed a golden aura around him and a halo on his head. He was surrounded by sheep, cows, and a crate of chickens. He walked over beer barrels to get to the shore.

"Forgive the disorder, Bishop," said the old sisters. "Since old Anton is gone, it's hard to keep things straight."

"How is the radish?" he asked.

"Poor, poor, Bishop. We pump all day, and the leaves still lie on the ground and don't want to stand up; the sand drinks the water—you can't expect the young girl to do it all alone—it's hard."

"I've missed you," he said. "You're my most faithful parishioners. I missed you in church—last Sunday."

They walked up through the radish field. "Look at them, Bishop. The radishes are in a bad way, the pump screeches like a wild beast, and we cannot go to church because the waters are too wild. We can't row through the Strudel."

"You need a man on the Island," said the Bishop. "You need a man to work and to get your boat through the Strudel."

"If only Anton were back. He was always quiet, he never seemed to do anything except play his guitar and sing, and yet he did all the work."

"We'll find somebody till he comes back," said the Bishop.

"Who could find anyone to come here and work, and live like this, Bishop?" said Saint Martha. "We can't offer him much—a bed and food, hard work, and little money."

"The Chaplain of the French prisoners of war will find someone," said the Bishop. "We will find a prisoner to come here and work on the Island."

The sisters' faces were filled with horror. They came forward and screeched together. "Oh, no, no, Herr Bishop —over our dead bodies—no, not a Frenchman—they are terrible people. The French, they smile at your face and then stab you in the back. You can't live with them. We'll be murdered in our bed at night."

"I'd rather jump into the Strudel," said Saint Anna. "A Frenchman—with a young girl on the Island. No, Bishop, thank you."

Saint Martha added, "They're funny people, the French."

"And so are the Kalmucks and the Americans and the Germans," said the Bishop. Their faces were still disturbed with thought of the calamity. "I'll go with you myself," said the Bishop, "and we'll look for a good Frenchman. How many years have you been on this Island?"

"Oh, I should say fifteen."

"Who owns it?"

"Nobody, Herr Bishop."

The Bishop exchanged his cane for the spade, and walked to the tip of the Island, to the point over which the Strudel sent its last rollers. He said that he had always wanted to put a small chapel there, a small chapel for a statue of St. Christopher, for the protection of boatmen and the souls of those who perished in the waves. He stuck the shovel into the ground, placed his foot on it, and turned the earth. With the two old sisters and the boatman as his aides and witnesses, he consecrated the ground and officially added the Island to his domain.

"Well, the silly Pfaff wants war, I'll give him war," said

the Gauleiter, who had been summoned to the tower the moment the barge had deposited the Bishop on the Island. The Gauleiter and the poet watched him leave it and sail down to the Walhalla. "Two can play that game," said the animal with the voice; "now it's our move. But this time we'll play it smartly. Without the Bureau of Licenses, and, if you don't mind, without your advice, Herr Assessor, we'll teach him a lesson. We'll do it on the Island, and right under the nose of the Pfaff." He pointed at his forehead. "I've got the plan. Watch out, Pfaff," he cried after the departing boat.

The Bishop stood at the portside of the boat and looked over the Danube at his cathedral as it sank among the roofs of the city and later came up again, when he was far enough down river. An hour later in Donaustauf he got off, and had to force money for his fare on the boatman. He walked up to the Walhalla, the German temple of fame built by Ludwig I of Bavaria—an edifice closely resembling the Parthenon in Athens. The Bishop paid the admission fee and put his shoes into the immense felt slippers that must be worn to protect the costly marble floor and entered the marble halls to see who remained of German great. Goethe was still there, Kepler the astronomer, Schiller, Nietzsche, and Wagner. Heine was absent, and Mendelssohn. In their places stood the statues of the Party's new personae gratae immortals. The Bishop walked out and wandered among the columns and waited until the small Walhalla train with the screeching wheels took him back to Stadt am Hof.

With cackling sounds and the expenditure of all his energy and affection, his small gray dog received him. He jumped up and down beside the big man as if he were suspended from a rubber band.

The next morning the Bishop, the sisters, and Leni were admitted at the prisoners' administration building by an old man. He seemed to be hanging at the side of the building as if held up by a coathook. His uniform, several sizes too large for him, hung in uncontrolled folds over his body, and much the same way hung the loose skin of his face. He pulled his shoulders up and scraped the heavy boots together, the heels of which were shod with iron like horses' hoofs. He saluted nicely for the Bishop, who knew him by name. The decrepit corporal, once retired and now doing guard duty, pointed the way to the door of the proper authorities, and the Bishop entered an office where two officials of the type of Ober-assessor Nebenzahl sat—two office creatures with inky fingers, elbow bands and paper cuffs to protect their shiny sleeves, parchment-colored men like two peculiar, long-legged bugs who climbed down from high chairs and listened to the Bishop with wishless, dead countenances, and then looked at each other, consulted a file, and searched in numerous books until the finger of one stuck on a line. He brought the book to the Bishop. "This one should do," he said. The prisoner's name was Paul Laprade; his religion, Catholic; his profession, stretcher bearer; his home, Lisieux. "You can't ask for more, your Grace," said the official, and wrote the prisoner's name on a piece of paper and handed it to a soldier as old and tired as the first, who took the Bishop and the three women through the building, past a gate and over a moat in

which some dogs barked, to a courtyard enclosed by ivy-covered walls.

The soldier disappeared, and they waited in the courtyard for a while. Eventually the man came back, handed the slip of paper to the Bishop, shook his head, and said simply, "I'm sorry, but he says that he doesn't want to come out."

"Wait here," said the Bishop. "We won't give up as easily as that. I shall go and talk to him myself."

The prisoner apologized to the Bishop. "Ah, no, dear Father," he said. "It is bad enough to be a prisoner of war, but being so, we are extremely grateful for the thickness of these walls. They keep us in, but they keep the swine outside. We cannot see them, thank God for that. We cannot even hear them." The young man was pale and underfed, his thin hands flew in a nervous gesture into his black hair. He then held them at his temples while he spoke. "You know, I haven't been out, we haven't seen any of them since we came here; and of those that are here, at the prison, we have seen only the boots, that is all, never their faces."

"It will do you good to go out," said the Bishop. "There is a plot of land, in the Danube, water all around you. The distance between the Germans and you is so great, they might be dwarfs or Chinamen. The scenery is lovely and three good people live on it. The work in the air will give you appetite and color, the smell of the earth will make you sleep, and to make things grow is one of the best medicines for the soul." The Bishop sat down on the prisoner's bed.

"To make things grow, to feed the pigs—" said the Frenchman. "Forgive me, dear Father, I have no longing for crude work in the fields, and their abominable potato cooking; we get enough of that here. As for the panorama, all of Regensburg or Germany that I wish to see appears in the hole in the green wall there. The clock on the bridgetower, we all sit and listen to it, and watch the time passing on it, and we wish we could make it spin."

"They are good people, Paul, those on the Island," said the Bishop. "I would not ask you to go there if they weren't. You will be better off on that island than you are here."

"We have our own island; dear Father, we have many islands. We go into this room at night and shut the door, so that no light from the half-blind lamp out in the corridor disturbs us. We lie down on our beds, and even in the darkness we close our eyes and fold our hands in back of our heads, and then one of the comrades begins to speak, and the islands that were our homes begin to appear before us. We were in Strassbourg last night, we were along the Quai Voltaire in Paris the night before that. We have, dear Father, exercised our memories so well that the smell of flowers, the sound of a cartwheel on a dirt road, the smallest details communicate themselves to us with miraculous clarity. I should miss it very much."

"Good, then, Paul," said the Bishop. "Good-by. Will you walk to the door with me?"

"But of course, dear Father," said the prisoner, and took his place on the left side of the Bishop and walked out into the courtyard.

"Those two are the ladies of the Island," said the

Bishop simply, pointing at Saint Anna and Saint Martha. The prisoner looked at them and then at Leni.

The Bishop walked across the courtyard to the two sisters and told them that the prisoner would come. The Frenchman stood still, his hands folded over the head of a stone lion who presided over the entrance. Leni said to the Bishop, "What is he waiting for?"

"I don't know," said the Bishop. "Oh, I forgot to ask him about something." He walked back. "I wanted to ask you a question," said the Bishop. "Are you familiar with boats?"

"With rowboats?"

"Yes, with rowboats."

"Yes, I can row a boat," said the prisoner. He paused, and then, looking at Leni, he said, "There are just women on the Island?"

"Yes, only women," said the Bishop.

"The young girl is with them?" asked the Frenchman.

"Yes, the young girl is with them."

"Of course I can row a boat—I row very well," said the prisoner. "I have not looked at people for years or talked to a woman. How elegant she is. This dreary place is suddenly bright—it feels like Sunday at home. Here is a serious question for me to answer, dear Father. May I think it over? At times it gets awfully lonesome here. The hours have leaden feet. Each day is gray, like the walls." He addressed it to the girl, who looked at him.

"Oh, you can decide at your leisure. No one will wish to force you. We can come again, or you may let me know through the Chaplain," said the Bishop.

"No," said the prisoner, "don't go away—let me think

now—" He folded his arm and turned around. He stayed so for a second and said, "I'll decide now. Do you mean, dear Father, that now I could go in, pack my six prunes, and leave this instant—go with you?"

"Yes, only first you must promise me that you will not try to escape, as I am responsible for you."

"Oh, if I go, I promise not to escape."

The prisoner had one hand in the mouth of the stone lion; with the other he rubbed his stubbly chin. He turned around; he wanted time only as an excuse to save some face. Behind him the Bishop said, with a smile on his face, "Let yourself be touched by pity."

With some degree of indifference, the prisoner said, "I am badly equipped to undertake a voyage, my attire is incomplete, all I have is this shirt, a scarf, the patched trousers of my uniform, and a cloak not much better. I shall not be at my best, but tell them, dear Father, that I will try to make myself useful, and to be patient with me. And now, if you will forgive me, I shall get my belongings and say good-by to my comrades."

The curious procession looked like a wedding. Crowds of people formed as they walked along; children ran in front of them. First came two soldiers and the prisoner, the Bishop and Leni followed, and in back of them trotted Saint Anna and Saint Martha. They marched over the bridge and through the beer garden, and took the barge to the Island.

C H A P T E R

8

WHILE the two old women listened as was required by the regulations, and the prisoner stood at attention looking straight ahead, one of the old soldiers rattled off the rules that govern prisoners of war who are assigned to work on farms. The soldier read:

The prisoner is to speak only when spoken to.

The prisoner is to be fed away from the family table.

He is to show himself three times a day to a patrol which passes along the quay.

The prisoner is to be paid the sum of forty pfennigs a day for his work.

The punishment for attempted escape is death and retribution exercised on the prisoner's comrades.

The punishment for incurring sex relations with German women is death and retribution exercised on the prisoner's relatives.

The punishment for a dozen other things was death and retribution. The guards determined at what part of the Island the prisoner was to show himself to the patrol. The hours and the nature of his work were written down and the sisters signed five copies of three sets of papers. They walked away, the patrol walked away, and the prisoner was left standing on grass, under the sky, close to the willow trees with the Danube rushing past, exactly as if he were a free man, to go anywhere he wanted to.

He stood there for a while and looked up at the bridge-tower. The Glockenspiel began to play, the golden statue of a child moved out toward a bell high up on the tower, the child's arm moved mechanically, and with a small hammer it sounded the quarter hour and disappeared. The face of the clock sparkled in the sunlight and the prisoner turned to look at the bridge, the village of Rein-hausen, the chalk cliffs along the Danube and the Wal-halla, and then he slowly walked toward the house. He wandered about, inspected the pump, walked to the boat, sat down in it, tried the oars and rowed for a while, set-ting the keel of the chained vessel into the current.

Since nobody seemed to want to talk to him, a plate of soup, bread, salt and pepper were placed on a table out-side the house. Beside the wobbly bench that stood there they had put a chair, and they watched from inside. It was as if they had brought a new, nice dog home, on whose every movement children's eyes hang for the first day. Leni carried some water out and put it on the table for him, and quickly ran into the house as he approached. "He's coming," she said. The sisters watched him eat. He was himself like the dog on the first day: he sniffed the air, came cautiously to the table, sat on the bench, with his back to the wall, and ate a few spoons of the potato soup.

"I'm afraid, even if he's good, he won't be much good for us," said Saint Anna. "Look what small hands and feet he has. I don't think he knows how to hold a shovel."

"He's pale and delicate," said Saint Martha, "and he promenades around like a young lord."

"If we don't get drowned, we'll end up down stream at the Walhalla. He'll never get us across the river, he'll never be able to fight the Strudel," they said, but they were no longer afraid of being murdered in their beds.

The prisoner sat outside. He looked around and saw them watching him through the window; he finished his soup, got up, and, like a beggar that has been fed, brought the empty plate to the pump, washed it out, and set it in the sun to dry, and then he came and asked them what he could do. Saint Martha said that for the first day he should just make himself at home and look around. As the sisters walked to the pump, he stood beside it and offered his hand to help them. As they stepped on the ladder he said, "Permit me, Madame," first to one and then to the other. After a while of pumping, and when the prisoner had wandered down to the radish field, they got over the surprise and smiled at each other. He was there again when they got down from the pump, offered his arm, and called each "Madame." The prisoner's courtesy ironed out their bitter faces for a moment, and when evening came they carried an extra sack of straw into the barn to put under his bed. They moved a bag of radish seed to another nail so that he could hang up his clothes, and gave him a lamp and a prayerbook, which was left opened at a page that showed a picture of the Grotto of Lourdes, and after they went back to the house and to bed, they sat up with worried faces and Saint Martha said, "Nobody has ever called me 'Madame.' He's so young and so polite."

"To me also he said 'Madame,' very seriously he said it, and he thanked me for the soup," said Saint Anna.

"And now he sits in his bed, all alone, without his mother, and far away from home. Oh, Lord, have pity on them all." Silently they folded their hands in prayer.

"To be lonesome, Martha, is the worst thing. Yes, that is the worst thing in all the world," said Saint Anna. She got up and wrapped a shawl around herself, walked out of the house, and opened the door of the barn. "Are you all right?" she said to the prisoner, who lay awake, his hands folded under his head.

"Yes, Madame," he said, "thank you. Good night, Madame."

In the morning the clumsy reception that honest people give one another took place all over again. The prisoner was up early, and the four stood for a while in the courtyard like the trees at the end of the Island, with no hands to extend to one another, their words inside of them. Nobody had shown the prisoner what to do. He ate and then rolled up his sleeves, took the heavy watering can, and carried it along the furthest row of radishes.

The pump began to work. Leni was at one end of the Island and the prisoner on the other; the two black birds sailed up and down; the radishes were watered in short time; and the prisoner began picking up dead branches. At the required intervals he walked along the shore presenting himself to the guard.

The second day he rowed the sisters across the Strudel. They held onto the sides of the boat as he started and they were sure he would drown them, but again they came out of it alive, and they brought him back a pack of cigarettes.

On the third day the tired, half-dead leaves of the

radish plants began to revive. They stretched themselves in the sun, their color came back, and they lifted themselves off the ground.

The sun shone, and after a week the radishes were completely recovered, and the sisters said, "The Bishop was right." They went to church and thanked God and the Bishop. At night they still sat up in bed and worried about the prisoner. "He's so grateful, so willing and so good," said Saint Anna. "I can't understand half the things he says, but I can't laugh when he says absurd things with his few words, it sounds so sad. I can't get over feeling that he is a little boy who is sent to bed. I can't look at him when he sits there with his piece of bread and thinks. I wonder what he thinks about."

"I know what he thinks about—about those that are not there—the way we think about Anton. He thinks about his father and his mother, his sisters and his brother, if he has any, what anybody thinks about, and his home town—he told me they had a river and a boat, like ours; and I'll cut his hair tomorrow, like I did Anton's. He excused himself today—he said he looked like a gypsy."

"Last week they cut his hair. This week he has a new shirt. Also, I must say," observed the poet in the beer garden, "the ladies of radish island are doing things in great style these days. Fresh as ever. For them there is no war, God is a good man in His Heaven, and everything is as it should be. You must visit the Island again, Herr Stolz. You would not recognize it. It's becoming as gay as the summer palace of the Duke of Thurn and Taxis, jollier than a merry-go-round. The prisoner is a cavalier and at the same time industrious as a bee, and inventive, too. He is at present amusing himself by building a little lattice garden house; he has already painted the boat in gay colors, and for the comfort of the passengers attached arm rests to the seats. The oars are decorated with candy stripes, ivy is planted at the foot of the pump, and a stairway leads up there now instead of a ladder, with handrails for the old crows—he'll tack a strip of red carpet to it next. At the end of the Island, the Bishop is building a little chapel for St. Christopher, and around this is a bed filled with forget-me-nots, which the prisoner has transplanted from the other end. That is not all. There is also a vegetable garden in which onions, asparagus, tomatoes, and string beans crowd each other. The diet at the place is changing, Herr Gauleiter, and people stop on the bridge and along the quay and admire the Island like a bouquet in a florist's window. The Frenchman fits into it like the fist on the eye. Toward evening the gypsies sit along the edge of their island and hang their feet in the water and sing. And everybody who sees it stops and laughs—and waves at them, and they wave back."

"I know," said the Gauleiter. "I've heard of that. Just wait, Herr Assessor. I'll give them something to laugh at."

"Oh, it's all in good order," said the poet. "They are very careful; so is the Bishop. All the regulations are observed. The Bishop's secretary filed the proper papers, all of them correct, a month ago, for the plan of a small chapel, made of materials that are on the Island, by volunteer work; the prisoner works after hours; the plans were submitted and had to be approved by the building department. Nothing is done that's against the law—

absolutely nothing. The prisoner sits on one end of the Island and the others sit on the other. Of course, what goes on at night, nobody knows."

The Gauleiter had a painful moment thinking of the night with the Frenchman and the young girl together on the Island—he was very sad. "We'll have to hurry," said the Gauleiter. "The Bishop is getting out of hand."

The poet agreed. "My relief man tells me that yesterday the old sacristan of the church of St. Emeram passed the Island and he waved over at the old crows and they waved back. The sacristan pointed up at the cathedral and shrugged his shoulders, as if to ask when they would come back to sell their radishes. They smiled and pulled a radish from the ground, and it was big and fat and snow white. And then the girl pointed at the prisoner and nodded with approval, and she swung her arms over the Island, showing how fine the radishes stood—it was like a barker inviting people to a fair."

"Wait, Pfaff," said the Gauleiter, "I'll give you music for your fair. I'll make your pets dance to another tune." He waved his fist toward the Island.

CHAPTER

9

THE sun was half-way up, between the two spires of the cathedral. Its rays leaned down over the gables of the Administration Building, sparkled in the golden Roman numerals of the clock on the bridgetower, and warmed the leaves of the radish plants. They were thick now and strong, and stood better than they had for a long time. The prisoner watered the last row, and when he was done he walked to the end of the Island, to the small chapel under the Apostle trees, and painted blue the niche into which a statue of St. Christopher was to be placed. It was a lovely morning. The girl stacked up the radish baskets.

The two old crows on the pump suddenly slowed down, and the hinge ceased yammering. Saint Martha was a little higher than Saint Anna; Saint Anna looked up the river. A ship was approaching the bridge on the placid side of the Danube. It was an unusual vessel, a curious conveyance. A rusty barge once used to dredge the river, it seemed too high to get through the arch of the stone bridge, but it was steered to the exact center, it made it, and emerged from the moist, thundering tunnel. As it came into the sunlight, a joyful shouting came from the throats of children. The hull of the boat was rusty, and a heavy, chain-draped mechanism to which mud scoops were attached rose from its center. Under a corrugated roof was a boiler, the controls that operated the scoop, and the steering platform. The ship was bedecked with bunting and gay flags; in the uppermost scoops sat little boys; in the lower scoops and all over the deck were boys and girls who hopped impatiently, climbed the dredge mechanism, and waved at the people on the bridge and on the Island as they passed it. Saint Anna and Saint Martha waved back at them and smiled, the children sang, the ship came out of the white foam of the Strudel, and the two old women began to look worried. As the dredge shot past the end of the Island it whistled. The man at the wheel strained his arms turning the wheel, he headed the craft into the quiet waters, and a few seconds later it came upstream and its iron keel buried itself in the mud. It was so old that the raised metal letters identified it as the dredge *Poseidon* of the Royal Bavarian Bureau of River Control, an authority that ceased to exist in 1918.

The engine stopped, and two youths in uniform, under the command of a teacher, jumped ashore. Planks were laid across the mud to the grass, whistles blew, shrill commands were shouted, a children's orchestra of flute, guitar, a drum and two concertinas marched ashore. In orderly rows, little boys and girls, two by two, holding hands, walked over the planks. A roll of canvas and some boards were brought ashore, and several tubs with milk and pink lemonade, baskets of rolls, pots with little sausages, cakes and pastry, were carried by little boys in uniform under the direction of the teacher, all with order and according to plan.

The teacher walked up toward the house and the pump, very polite to the old crows, and selected the courtyard as the place where he wanted a stand to be assembled. It was done with dispatch and efficiency; in a short while everything was in its place and decorated with bunting and with flags.

Gauleiter Stolz waited until after twelve to escape the worst clanging of the ancient clock on top of the tower. Then the animal with the voice dragged himself up the sixty-nine steps. He was sweaty and breathed through his mouth as he came up, sounding as if someone was beating against the inside of an empty barrel. He rested on the last platform, outside the clock's mechanism, while the poet, beside himself with admiration, talked down to him through the trap door that opened out on the gallery of the tower. "Also," said the poet, "I think it was purest genius on your part, Herr Gauleiter. The Bishop himself couldn't have done better. 'Suffer little children to come unto me,' it says. The Pfaff can't complain about that— sunshine and fun for a children's outing. It's a feast for the eyes of a saint. My most respectful compliments, my unreserved admiration, Herr Gauleiter. Here, take the gun, you'll see better."

The Gauleiter climbed the last steps and hung his cane on the banister. "Ah—" he said, and squinted with one eye as he looked through the telescopic sight of the gun. "What fun the little ones are having. The real fun, Herr Assessor, begins at twelve-thirty. Here is the program, Herr Assessor. Read. Everything is going according to schedule."

Below, the small children stood around their teacher and looked up at the tower, while the teacher pointed with his cane and explained the clock to them. "From here, dear children, we enjoy the best view of the tower clock. I want your closest attention now—look at it. It is regulated for a thousand years. It indicates the sixty seconds of the minute, the sixty minutes of the hour, the twenty-four hours of the day, and the twenty-eight days of the moon. It is so wonderful that it shows the phases of the moon, the eclipses of the sun, and the position of the earth in every season. On the thirty-first of December, at midnight, it rings a yearly change, a new date appears, and remains fixed until the next thirty-first of December. From six in the morning to six of the evening, a graceful, small child appears and rings the quarter hour, a young man armed with an arrow strikes the half hour, and an old man with a scythe, the full. But what is the most remarkable thing about this clock, who can tell me?" He pointed at the most eager boy. "You, Rudolph Unruh, tell us."

"That it is set for a thousand years."

"And why is that the most remarkable and wonderful attribute of this clock?"

"Because it will measure the time of greatest glory for the Fatherland."

"Well said, very well said. We shall now sing a song," said the teacher. "Where are the musicians? Also, we shall sit down in the shade. Also, let's go—one, two, three—"

The children below sat in a ring, under the Apostle trees, the teacher in the center, and they sang children's songs. The teacher conducted the orchestra. It was then twelve-thirty, the golden statue of the man with the arrow came out of the tower, the animal with the voice held his ears, and the poet opened his mouth as the clock struck the half hour. "Now the games," said the teacher below, and pointed at a small girl with carrot red hair. "You," he said, "you're it." He took a black bandage out of his pocket and blindfolded the child and took her by the hand, walking up the path. Until then, the children had carefully stayed on the paths and along the rim of the Island. Now, the teacher spun the little girl around several times and let her loose. She stumbled into the radishes, and the game was played over the field where the best ones grew.

One of the older boys in uniform began drilling the six-year-olds. He ordered them into ranks, he deployed them. "Eins, zwei, drei," he yelled at them. The battalion went through its formations, up and down, over the Island, and the second field of radishes was trampled.

There was a pole with ribbons attached to it for the girls to dance around, and the teacher stuck it into the third patch. For the fourth, the teacher threw a football in the air; the children did the rest.

The prisoner stood motionless and looked at the clock. The old sisters sat with folded hands at the table, and said to Leni, "Quiet, child, don't cry. Don't cry, baby, don't cry. It will pass."

Up on the tower the Gauleiter reached into his coat and brought a package to light. He opened a combination bottle opener and pocket knife, sat on the topmost step of the stairs that led down to the clock, and unpacked two hard-boiled eggs, a Regensburger Knackwurst, a slice of Swiss cheese, and two cones made of tiny pieces of newspaper,

from which he shook salt and pepper on his food. The beer he drank out of the bottle.

The sausages and the kraut below were heated; the children lined up. The teacher came and supervised the feeding. After the repast, the children discovered the pig and chased it all over the Island.

Up on the tower, the Gauleiter said, "An outing like that, once a month, will do a lot for those poor children." The poet had unwrapped a roll with a slice of liver sausage and ate it, leaning out over his tower. He looked down the Danube and noticed the barge from Donaustauf being pulled upstream by the two percherons. He picked up the gun and looked through the telescopic sight, and, turning, he said, "Sorry to disturb you, Herr Gauleiter, but come here and take a look—and see who is coming. Now it's getting interesting—very. Look who's coming. Look down toward the Walhalla." Standing in the barge, the Bishop of Regensburg approached slowly, his chancellor with him, holding the wooden statue of St. Christopher like a baby in his arm. The stout horses steadily pulled the vessel upstream—the barge was a mile away— when the teacher blew his whistle and ended the visit. As orderly as they had come, the visitors left the Island. The planks were drawn in, the music played, and the rusty hulk of the *Poseidon* withdrew from the devastated island. It backed up into the placid water, churned the mud, and slowly turned and moved out into the Strudel. On top of the two metal beams that supported the chains and buckets of the dredge, a large Party flag had been attached, and it was waving in the wind. It slowly moved past the Island, and the children, warm and untiring, climbed around the boat, sat in all the iron buckets like birds in their nests, and waved their gratitude at the Island.

"Your move now, Pfaff," said the Gauleiter on the bridgetower. Music played, the children sang. The old iron dredge wallowed through the foam and over the waves of the Strudel; the bunting at its side was soaked. The man at the wheel maneuvered in the cross currents and headed for the fifth arch. The ship labored under full steam, and the teacher sent someone up on the top to take the flag down so that the ship could pass under the arch without injuring the Party emblem. The boy on the top of the beam loosened the flag and handed it down to a comrade below. He was half-way down the beam when the boat rose, swayed slowly, turned sideways, and hesitated for a minute. The children all stumbled to starboard and dangled from the scoops. Then the old iron dredge turned quietly over, gulped, and began to sink. The people on the bridge were silent for a second and then shrieked. The roar of the water drowned the cries of the children; a few pairs of little arms reached out of water; the hull drifted toward the Island. At the quay, boats were made loose, two brave men jumped directly from the bridge into the Strudel, and each one saved a child. The prisoner ran to the tip of the Island, dove into the water, and brought three of them out. But the swift currents of the Danube carried most of them out into the middle of the stream, rushed them past, and brought them to shore near the Walhalla three days later.

Those that were taken from the water lay with cramped

little fingers in the grass among the small flowers. The small golden child on the clocktower rang the bell, and those below that crawled on land stank of the mud, and stood and sat about with their teeth chattering, their knees knocking, their faces blue.

Little Rudolph Unruh wept for his teacher. The Policeman Umlauf dived again and again, and dragged children from the scoops of the dredge, but by now it was too late for those he brought on land. The old sisters bedded them in grass and covered them. The Bishop knelt at their sides and prayed.

The prisoner rowed the lightest loads to shore that he had ever taken from the Island.

It was printed in the *Regensburger Anzeiger* that the excursion had been arranged by the teacher, who was also the leader of the Youth Movement, and who was among the casualties.

The Gauleiter sold black-bordered handkerchiefs by the dozen, the poet rhymed some words into a touching and suitable obituary, and three musical instruments were washed ashore on the Island. The funerals were performed quietly, the Danube flowed past as it always had, and St. Christopher, who had arrived an hour late, stood in his chapel and marked the watery grave.

CHAPTER
10

"WHY do you always look at the clock?" Leni had said to the prisoner on one of the first days that he was on the Island, as they met working on a row of radishes. He looked at her a long while before answering, and then he worked alongside of her and said, "I watch it, I watch it every day. I looked at it through the loop-hole of the prison for two years, because I know that sometime, at six at night, or at three in the morning, when the hands point up or to the right—but at an hour that will appear there, as this hour does now—it will be over, and there will be an end to it. And now, while the hands slowly turn there, my friends are coming, they are getting ready in thousands of ships, with cannon and planes, nearer and nearer, to end this disgrace. That, Mademoiselle, is why I am always looking at that clock, the only beautiful thing here in Regensburg." Beyond polite greetings, and thanking her for the food she brought him or to ask her to help him with the lattice work or his flowers, they had not spoken again until after the children's visit. But ever since then he was near where she was, within the limit of distance prescribed by the regulations.

The Bishop came again the day after the disaster. "Take the radishes," he commanded, "trampled as they are, wash them, and put them into baskets, row them across on Sunday, and sit at the cathedral as usual."

There were two troopers in uniform and with note-books outside the door of the church, the Gauleiter cruised about in front of the cathedral and the poet watched from the tower; but all the ruined, bruised radishes were sold.

The pump stood still for two days after that, as they planted the last crop before the floods would come. The bow of the *Poseidon* stuck out of the Strudel at the end of the Island like the nose of a shark; the water gurgled in the empty hull; otherwise all was as it had been before. The prisoner presented himself to the patrol toward evening; the swallows traced their course from the roofs of buildings down through the tunnels of the bridge, folded their long, tailcoat-like wings and shot down to within inches of the surface of the Danube, hunting the insects that hovered over the mirror-like surface. Then they soared upward over the Strudel to their nests on the gables and towers of Regensburg, and, as the bells of the cathedral pealed for the Ave, the city began to go to sleep.

For a while the playing of children echoed in the darkening streets, a few lamps were lit, and then all became quiet except the clock. After the clock on the bridge tolled nine, the prisoner came from his barn and walked to the house. Like a doctor, he listened for the intake and outtake of air in the beds of the old crows, for the wheezes, coughs, rasping, and whistling that came from the room of the holy sisters. He waited until they changed to the even rhythm of their snoring, and then he walked to the side of the house, whistled like a bird, and leaned his shoulder against the house until Leni's left foot was firmly placed on it. He cupped his hand for the right foot in front of him, and as her knees were pressed against his chest, he let her go, to catch her under the arms. "Au revoir, in five minutes," he said, and they walked separately until they met at the end of the Island. They sat there in the shadow of the Apostle trees, two feet away from each other, looking down over the water to an inlet in which the slow current of water forever twisted the round leaves of water plants. Beyond the trees across the river was a house with lettering on it. The word "American" still shone through the cheap paint with which it had been covered. Below that appeared in large red letters the word "Dentist." The "D" in dentist framed a window, out of which every evening, resting on a pillow, the dentist blew smoke into the air. He stared into the dark for an hour after his precious cigarette was smoked and then closed the window and went to bed. The light from his window shone across and gilded the whitecaps at the end of the Strudel, lit up the last swells of the river, and melted away in foam and wave.

The prisoner rested his back on the tree, and Leni sat two feet away from him. It took three weeks before they reached for each other's hand. He made her familiar with his landscape and his people; he talked of his work and of his parents' house. Her eyes became moist whenever he spoke of himself. She did not understand everything he said—he had picked up English, Spanish, and Italian words along with the German from the babel of tongues that is Lourdes, and in his difficulty to express himself he mixed foreign words with the wrong German words. As a stretcher bearer he had heard German pilgrims ask for "ein Kissen," which is a pillow, and from American films at the Cinéma Musée de Bernadette he had picked up the word "kiss," which he learned was the word one used when desiring to embrace another; and in the first conversation about love, which took place in the fifth week of their acquaintance, he became mixed up and asked whether he might give her a "Kissen." Leni said that she was comfortable enough without one, but a while after the silence that followed, she leaned her head toward his and told him that "Kuss" was the word. He had kissed her then, on the eyes, on her forehead, on her hands, on her cheeks, and the grass was crushed where they had sat. But after that he never kissed her again. "They are in the way, over there, Leni," he said, "in the compound, the comrades in the dark room."

"Paul, oh, Paul," she said, "I've kissed you every night ever since you came."

"'Kissen' is the right word, Leni. I've kissed my pillow every night before I went to sleep."

"I do the same, Paul."

"But if I were to say one word of love or marriage to you, I would die of shame—until they're free to do the same, until we're all free, until I come back for you."

"It's good as it is, poor Paul. Only not to be alone—only not to be without you."

"Until I came, Leni, I was secure in prison. I did not feel anything like the hurt I have now. I have been lonely from that day I came here. There was but I—over in the citadel. I was, like the others, a dead man who had sad dreams. You and this isle have brought me back, and brought my home back; and when I sit alone here at the table and eat, they are all about me. It is like the evening at home during the winter months, when we were all seated at dinner around the table, under the lamp, in the house at the side of the small river, and the dog cruising in back of us, going from place to place in search of food. Outside in the dimness was a clocktower and the time on it, like the one over there—not as grandiose a mechanism, but the hour bells sounded like yours do here. And here on this isle I built a little sunhouse like our own that seemed so warm when you looked at the cold ground outside. My father was an honest man, my mother dead, and my little sister Madeleine took her place. Leni, oh, Leni, where is she and where is my old father? What has happened to them, to the house, and the old dog?" He seemed ill, he trembled. "Leni, you are," he said, and cramped her hands in his and pressed his head against her, "my little sister Madeleine." He looked up to the stars. "Protect her, oh, God. Look after her, dear Lord. She's one of your best children." He wept then. "I pray that I may die first, that I may plead with God for you who have loved me like a mother, dear sister. I would give my eyes, my ears, my voice for you, and if I should have to lose my arms and still live on, I should do so joyfully for your sake." He was in a fever; he talked wildly after that. She walked back with him and sat at the side of his bed until the daylight came. He was in a fever for several days, and for much of that time delirious.

When he was well again, during the second conversation about love, she said, "Paul, I have thought often about the death of soldiers in war, I have always wanted to find some consolation. I said to myself, people die any-

way. We all have to die, and some would die as horribly in peace as in war, in accidents and of painful diseases. And then I thought, if but one woman's son is killed in war, in this mother's heart there is all the sorrow that is in this world. If it's two mothers or a hundred or a thousand or more, it is all the same—it's only one mother's grief repeated, and therefore, as sorrow goes, no more than that of the first, and the difference is only more funerals, more coffins—the difference is economic."

They were silent for a while. "No," said Paul, "you're wrong. You mustn't talk like that. You almost talk like they do, Leni."

"Tell me if it's otherwise, Paul," she said. "Oh, the first son might have been a great doctor, and the second one killed a musician, and the third just a good man, or a brewer—a man like old Anton or the Bishop—and the more of them die, the colder the world becomes and the poorer, and all that will be left are the men who stand at the side of graves with shovels in their hands."

"No, Leni, love is stronger than death, and that is what will save us. If it weren't, Leni, it would have been cold here on earth long ago, and you and I would not be here. When you say that one such sorrow is the sorrow of all the world, I say that one love is all the world's love, it burns like the small candles before the old women in the cathedral, and it warms and shines, and because it is beautiful and good and because death is cold, more and more light their fire on the one small light, until the earth is bright again and like the heavens filled with stars. That is how it is."

On that night the dentist across the river retired early

—it was eleven. He stood up in his lighted window and stretched himself, and took the pillow on which he leaned as he looked out from the window sill and closed the window. The protective beam of light, in which any approaching boat could have been seen, was gone.

The next night Leni said, "I've thought about what you said yesterday. You are right, Paul. That's how it is, and since it is that way, the gravediggers are guilty, and they are those that bring it on, and those that are guilty and have done it, and they will be forever hated. Oh, they will try and explain, and change into other clothes, but no one will believe them. It is as if a woman stops loving a man. He can stand on his head, he can put on another uniform with gold and all the shiny medals he can wear, and come with gifts and flowers and talk nicely—it's over with and done, and nothing that he can do will ever change her heart."

Over on the quay a battalion of Party members, fat men, marched and sang. Paul looked at them. "Gross, stupid race, and in their midst only a few handful that dare revolt. What idiocy it took to choose the man they follow. Once, Leni, long ago, I traveled with my father. We were on a walking tour through Austria, and we came to an inn in a small town late at night. My father rang the night bell and the door opened, and a pale, tired night porter with a green billiard cloth apron opened the door and let us in. He carried our bags upstairs and placed them on the floor, and then he picked up shoes from in front of the doors of the guests and with chalk he wrote the room number on the soles. He was very tired, stupid, and unpleasant. He wore a little mustache, and that is how he seems to me, the man who leads them on—the pale night porter of the dirty inn." The shaft of the light from the dentist's window died in a patch of the blossoms of buttercups that were in bloom that night, and they went back.

The prisoner was well again, his heart secure and his honor anchored to promises they had given each other. In two lessons that followed in two nights, he taught her the words of an old French song. Leni was singing it slowly the third night when, although neither of them had an instrument, the song was suddenly accompanied by a guitar. The singing stopped. The leaves of the bushes in front of them moved. They sat still while the head of a man emerged from the greenery.

"Shh," said the accompanist, "it's only me." Old Anton's face looked up at them. He showed them his old hat, into which he had stuck twigs and branches. "I came back three days ago from a voyage to Vienna."

"Uncle Anton!"

"Shh, be quiet. I thought at first he was one of them," he said, nodding toward the prisoner and pointing with his thumb at the city. He held up the guitar. "I found this only yesterday there in the mud and cleaned it. I couldn't stand it any more, I had to come back. But I'll go away again. Don't tell anybody you saw me."

"Poor Uncle Anton—" said Leni.

He sat on the grass beside them. "I've got to talk, I'll talk quietly, and then I'll go and hide myself again."

"You come and stay in the barn at night, and in the daytime you can hide here in the bushes," said Leni.

"Bushes or barn—oh, I'm glad I'm back. I lived under

a bridge in Vienna; I talked with people there," said Anton, "and I was hungry."

"But they're kind, the Viennese," said the prisoner. "Everyone knows about the golden Viennese heart—"

"Oh, the golden Viennese heart. Let me tell you about that," said Anton. "There was a fellow who fed me, under the bridge—you always find somebody, someone like yourself. He was an Austrian and in deep trouble. He told me about the Viennese golden heart. He said that it was an old story, but that the Viennese heart is still as golden. There was once a poor little old woman, he said, who had lost her only treasure, her last hope and joy, her only son. And she walked down to the Danube, and sat on the bank of the river for a while crying all alone, and then she took her shoes off, and slowly walked down into the Danube. Just then a policeman came, dressed in a beautiful uniform with a shiny helmet, and he stopped and said in his soft Viennese dialect, 'What are you doing there, little old mother?' And she said, 'I am a poor old woman, I have nothing to live for any more, and I am going to walk into the Danube and drown myself.' 'But, little mother,' said the policeman, who had a typical Viennese golden heart, 'you mustn't do that—you can't go into the Danube. If you go into the Danube, I must jump after you and I'll get my beautiful uniform wet. Go home, little mother,' he said, 'go home and hang yourself instead.' Ah, the poor Danube—she is different there, she is a stranger. I wandered alongside of her, I sat and watched her, I became so lonesome that I put my feet into the water, like the little old mother, and I closed my eyes and thought that the water that flowed past my feet had, a while ago, run past this island. You don't know, my children, what it is to be away from home."

"Is it blue in Vienna, the Danube?" asked the prisoner.

"No, not any more than it is here, but about that my friend under the bridge also told me a story. He said that when the great composer who wrote *The Blue Danube* was a little boy, his mother was very poor, and she bought him a blue suit. The blue suit was very cheap, and it got dirty, and the mother went down to the Danube to wash it. The little boy sat beside her, and in the water the dye ran out of it and for a moment the Danube was blue. And in memory of that, the great composer named his waltz 'The Blue Danube.' "

"If one waits long enough, there is an explanation for everything," said the prisoner.

"I'm hungry!" old Anton shouted.

"Pss! Shh!" said Leni. Leni went to the house to get some food for old Anton.

The old man played with a stick for a while, then he tapped the prisoner's shoulder with it and pointed through the fifth arch of the bridge. "In the daytime," he said, "when you look through the fifth arch of the bridge, you see large trees there, a garden full of them, a beer garden called The Blue Danube. That," he said, "at one time belonged to me. I'm Anton Fischer, I'm a brewer."

"Yes, Monsieur," said the prisoner, "I know of you," and offered his hand. "Paul is my name, Paul Laprade. I was a stretcher bearer in Lourdes once."

"It wasn't always like this with me," said the old man. "I was once a respected man. There's only one who remembers my sisters and me there, and treats us with re-

spect—an old woman who worked for us. She's still there
—Frau Saltner is her name. When she was young, when
those trees there were half as big as they are now, times
were different. The beer was sold for twenty pfennigs a
liter, the hops and malt five marks a hundredweight, and
my property was assessed at fifty thousand marks. You
knew where you stood. I sold the brewery when the infla-
tion came. I couldn't keep up with it any more. We had
a black tablet hanging on a tree and on that Frau Saltner,
who was a young girl then, wrote with white chalk what
the price of food and drink was. The price changed every
hour—it was telephoned to the city hall from Berlin—
and sometimes a Schnitzel that was a million and a half
marks when the customer ordered it, had gone up to two
million when he wiped his mouth and asked for the bill.
So it was with everything, and then one day they offered
me fifty billion marks for the property, and I thought it
couldn't get any worse. I was half crazy, and so was everybody else, and I was tired, so I sold out and I took the
money to retire. A month after, the fifty billion marks
that I got for the beer garden barely bought a straw hat.
The enemy didn't do it, our Government did it; and
everybody lost his property, and we all became paupers.
The rich saved themselves, but all the small people with
savings and small property were ruined, and with small
property went honor and self-respect, and that was the
time when honest men became rare, and that was when
he arrived to save us—you know who I mean.

"I was lucky. I had a gold mine in a cellar that was cut
into the lime cliffs near Reinhausen, right at the foot of
the Walhalla. We lagered the beer there, and in this

cellar I had almost two hundred brand-new beer barrels, and on those we lived, selling one a week. They rose like balloons in price, but that also came to an end. The cave was empty, my gold mine was gone, there were five broken barrels left, and with those broken old ones we moved to the Island and planted radishes. You can see those barrels standing in a row here on the Island. We sold the radishes at the entrance to what once was our own property, and they're funny, people. The Regensburgers, they all forgot us—it was Herr Fischer this, Herr Fischer that, when we had the beer garden—they suddenly stopped saying good day. For a while they stood still as they walked in, and looked at Anna and Martha as at two old dogs lying at the entrance to the garden. All but Frau Saltner and the Bishop forgot us. And only once in my whole life I spoke up and told them, and then I had to leave. And it's the same all down the valley, in every hamlet, in every city. And in Austria, it's the same."

"It's terrible," said the prisoner, "but you're in your own land, and if enough of you choose, you could take them and shake them the way dogs shake rabbits, break their necks, and throw them away. And anyway, you're still fortunate. There's one thing that can't happen to you, and that is, the Germans can't march in on you."

"They've marched in on us a long time ago," said old Anton. "One kind of Germans marched in on the other. They talk of secret weapons—if only somebody would invent a gun that misses decent people and shoots at the others."

"What happened to the beer garden?"

"Ah, a foreigner, a man from Ulm, by the name of

Anspacher, came and bought it, and he couldn't make it go. You have to be born here, you have to know the people to make a beer garden go. He lost it, and then came the Party—they are very fond of beer cellars, beerhallen, and beer gardens. They're to them what the cathedral is for the Bishop. And now it belongs to them, it's administered by the Party, the Herr Gauleiter is one of the directors. I guess one of these days he'll say it belongs to him, now that Oberassessor Nebenzahl is out of the way."

"Old Anton is under the Apostle trees," said Leni to the old crows, "and during the day he's down at the end of the Island in the bushes." The old sisters took a walk the next evening toward the tip of the Island, and they stopped and talked to the trees. "God greet you, Anton," they said. "Is there anything we can bring you?" And the bush in which he sat answered, "Oh, God, Anna and Martha, you know I have a terrible hunger for something good to eat. All kinds of wonderful things appear before me. I can feel them and smell them—a veal stew, for example, a rabbit, a roast goose, a ham—" said old Anton in his bush. "Particularly a roast goose. If I could only have a roast goose either cold or warm—oh, God—the way we had it at the brewery. If I could get that, I would be very happy and forever grateful."

"Nothing less than goose, he must have," said Martha. "Well, a pork cutlet—then. What happened to the pig?"

"The pig is fine," said Saint Anna. "Quiet, lay low, Anton, don't get too fresh. Don't sit out in the sun. We saw you from the pump today. Keep quiet, hide, Anton, until we tell you, or they'll come for you. Where will we get a goose from? We can't stand on the tip of the Island and wait until one comes floating like the pig did, but you just say, 'I want a goose,' and open your mouth waiting for it to fly in."

"If he wants a goose," said Leni, "he shall have one. We'll go to Reinhausen; we'll go from one farm to the other and tell them it's for old Anton; and we'll get a goose, and pay for it, and cook it."

And so the two sisters got up earlier than usual and pumped, and then they got into their boat and the prisoner rowed them to Reinhausen.

CHAPTER

11

THE old beer garden was like the neglected child of an alcoholic—the trees unkempt, the orchestra shell stacked with broken chairs, part of the fence washed away.

Frau Saltner placed a plate of goulash and some bread before the air-raid warden. She breathed as if she had run up three flights of stairs. She brought the beer, dragging her feet through the parched leaves of the chestnut trees that scraped across the sand in the wind. The wetness of the Danube came up over the tables and coated the chairs and the trees.

At the table next to the Assessor sat a woman, old, docile, and unintelligent. Her lips, affected by a nervous disorder, moved in a way that gave her the look of a rabbit chewing. The woman's eyes were on her son whose hands she covered with her own. A gust of wind brought movement into the trees and dropped a few black twigs on the ground.

The Gauleiter came into the garden. He honored the hero in the wheelchair with a special salute. The soldier looked away. His mother, instead, nodded respectfully. The young soldier talked to his mother, looking straight ahead. Her mouth stopped twitching. She mumbled something to her son and got up, and pushed the wheelchair away from the Gauleiter's table to the music shell.

The young man looked at the faded panorama in the shell, and at the Danube that was gray and dirty. His mother's mouth was chewing again. She wiped the boy's face with her handkerchief. The sun between the clouds warmed him, and now that he was away from the table, one could see that he was without legs.

"Sorry to be late, Herr Assessor," said the animal with the voice after the salute and the manly handshake.

"Can you tell me, Herr Gauleiter, what rhymes with Rommel?" said the poet. "I have passed the time writing, if you please, Herr Gauleiter."

He handed a piece of paper to his bloodbrother, who read:

> *The Eisenhower, The Eisenhower*
> *That is a particularly schlauer,**
> *In Deutschland any potato-Bauer,†*
> *Is as schlau as this Eisenhower,*
> *We have our good Rommel—*

"That is where I am stuck," said the poet. "Something to go with Rommel—"

"It should be easy," said the animal with the voice. "Let's think."

The poet's eyes wandered over the bridge and along the houses on the waterfront for a while. They searched for a word to rhyme with Rommel.

The poet, chewing the end of his pencil, pointed at the Island.

"Oh," he said, "I have news, Herr Gauleiter. At last something is happening over there. The gypsies are busy

* *Schlauer*—clever.
† *Bauer*—peasant.

like a swarm of bees." He pulled the sleeve of the Gauleiter. "I would not be surprised if at last we could move
in there and take the Island over sooner than we expected. The Bishop's pets are getting a celebration together."

"Trommel rhymes with Rommel," said the animal
with the voice.

"Thank you, Herr Gauleiter."

He drew a primitive sketch of a drum on the piece of
paper.

"Drum is an excellent martial word—goes well with
Rommel. My respects, Herr Gauleiter. How about:

> *But we have our good Rommel,*
> *He'll play a tune upon his Trommel—?*

"Tell me more about the Island," said the Gauleiter.
"Just a minute," said the inspired poet. "How is this:

> *Wait, Eisenhower, until our Rommel,*
> *Stretches your hide across his Trommel—?*

The Gauleiter looked toward the Island. He was impatient. "Not bad," he said. "What about the Island?"

"Well, I shall find the proper rhyme up there in my
tower tonight," said the poet, and put the pencil and
paper away.

"To come to the Island, I have here the various reports of my relief men. It seems that one of them noticed
something was wrong when the pump stood still one
morning. He kept the Island under close surveillance
from then on. Here is the picture which shapes up from

my own observations and those of the Party members
Huber and Sinz who relieve me.

"Day before yesterday the pump was idle at nine, indi-
cating something was wrong. As I have stated before, the
Island was kept under the closest surveillance. The sisters
Fischer appeared at the door of their house at ten-thirty
and walked to the Danube, where the prisoner waited beside the boat. He rowed them across the Strudel to Reinhausen. They returned from there at noon with a goose.

"They resumed pumping at three, and nothing unusual happened for the rest of the day.

"The next day, the goose was taken out to be killed,
but escaped from one of the sisters. The other sister, the
young girl, and the prisoner joined in the chase. The
goose was headed for the Danube, and was finally caught
by the prisoner who gave it to one of the sisters. It was
killed sometime between twelve and one, and the young
girl was busy plucking it."

The Assessor looked from his paper to the Gauleiter,
expecting approval. "I try to keep in mind what happened before. I know that we must proceed with utmost
care—" said the poet.

"So far," said the animal with the voice, "you haven't
told me anything that is worth anything. Peasants visit
peasants and return with a goose. That's quite natural.
It's a church holiday, so they cook the goose and eat it.
Nothing in that to get excited about."

"Ah," said the poet, "you are right. I am coming to
that. That's precisely it. They've celebrated like that before, but not this time. Follow me. Say they wanted to

celebrate. They would have eaten at noon—they always eat at noon. A goose takes a good while to cook. If it had been in the oven for several hours, there would have been a fire, and where there is a fire, there is smoke. But there was no fire this morning. The goose is not cooked yet. I have my own thoughts about it—it looks suspicious to me."

"Bah," said the Gauleiter, "you don't know these people. If they have a goose, they won't keep it. They won't even keep the grease. They'll pluck it and clean it and lay the slab of fat on the breast, and then place it on green leaves, and you know who will get it—his Eminence, the Bishop, or some other Pfaff."

"There is more, Herr Gauleiter," said the poet, "if you'll allow me to continue:

"So, today, they stop pumping again at nine, and the prisoner is waiting with the boat, and the two old crows wander down to the water. The prisoner holds their hands as they sit down. He is like a chauffeur. It's all elegant, like plutocrats going for a ride in a gondola in Venice. He rows them through the Strudel, and now the ladies walk up to the Neupfarrplatz, and, unashamed, they enter the pastry shop of Obergruppenführer Keppelmayer.

"Party member Sinz calls up as soon as he sees them come out of the door with a package. He is told that they bought a cake.

"From there, they go to the wine merchant Himmelstoss in the Lederergasse, and leave that shop with two bottles of wine.

"What for do the swine need wine?" said the poet.

"But that is not all. They are followed with the binoculars and isn't it most peculiar that they stop at the department store? There they bought a Japanese paper lantern.

"The total expenditure for these items, as checked by telephone, was eight marks and twenty pfennigs.

"From the department store, they went to the Carmelite church—I suppose to have the cake and the lamp and wine blessed by the Pfaffen. They remained there for half an hour, and then they went back to the Danube.

"Now, I am waiting to see what will happen. Why don't you pay a visit to the Island, Herr Gauleiter, this afternoon, just in the normal routine of duty? You might see something."

"If there is anything in what you tell me, I would warn them. They will take heed and we'll spoil the work you've done. Lie low and keep on watching them closely."

"Herr Gauleiter," said the poet, sitting up straight, pressing his buttocks together, "I will be most grateful if it is learned in the right places that Assessor Unruh does his work thoroughly, untiringly, far beyond the point of duty, and uncomplaining!"

"Results are what count, my good Assessor," said the Gauleiter. "You are expected to do your duty to the last breath that is in you, like the soldier in the field. The Führer and Deutschland expect that from the highest and the lowest of us."

"I can do no more," whined the Assessor. "I am already an air-raid warden, a loyal Party member from the beginning of the movement, contribute to everything, pay my taxes; yet I remain a plain assessor, in spite of the fact that, since the incompetent Oberassessor Nebenzahl has been removed, I have done the work of an Ober-assessor. Since I have the years, since I am entitled to the advancement to the post, and since I have the responsibility, why not the title?"

The Gauleiter took the Assessor's arm—he had not listened to him—and pointed at the Island which he had been watching.

"Ah, ah, ah," said the Gauleiter. His face lit up. A thin wisp of smoke came out of the chimney.

"Look, Herr Assessor, the goose is cooking," he said.

He took out his watch and compared it with the clock on the bridgetower. It was almost half-past three. He called for the bill. The waitress came to the table.

"Tell me, Frau Saltner, how long does it take to roast a goose?" asked the Gauleiter.

"Ja, half an hour to get the oven properly hot, and then three hours, I should say."

"Ah," said the Gauleiter, "the Gypsies—they're becoming truly elegant. They eat late, after dark like high society."

On the way over the bridge, they stopped and watched the smoke rise over the Island.

"Herr Assessor, maybe you have something there. But this time extreme caution!" said the Gauleiter. "We shall see. Keep me informed."

At the end of the bridge, before he walked up to his tower, the Assessor once more voiced his request.

"May I, dear Herr Gauleiter, once more most respectfully lay my request at your door? Old Party member, two sons at the front, veteran of the last war, unquestioned loyalty—"

"Yes, yes, yes," said the Gauleiter. "We know all about you. We shall see what can be done."

Herr Unruh went home to don his Party uniform and then went to relieve the man on the tower.

The smoke from the Island drifted slowly down over the Danube. During the next two uneventful hours, the poet successfully rhymed Rommel with Trommel, and after that the failing light blurred his efforts.

The machinery of the clock in the dusty room beneath his feet began to work. The steady ticktock rhythm of the huge pendulum was lost while a drum started to turn. A whirring sound was followed by a mechanical tapping like the sounds of an old typewriter amplified. Wires strained and pulled and over the air-raid warden's head, the hammers rose. Pigeons and swallows left the tower and sailed out over the Danube, and the hammers fell. The poet held his ears and opened his mouth. The structure shook as the large bell was struck. The hands on the four dials on the outside of the tower proclaimed that it was six o'clock.

The pigeons came back to the tower, and Assessor Unruh picked up the phone and made his routine report to Headquarters. He looked over the city through his binoculars.

Regensburg is like a huge set of old teeth clamped against the river—a semicircle of ancient walls, bastions, and battle towers. Within this medieval stone embrace, house crowds house. The narrow streets run like rivulets to the few squares, which are faced by government buildings, the theater, churches, and breweries. A building commission has kept the street picture harmonious. All new construction has had to conform to the mood of the existing architecture, and therefore all the houses are gabled, the pavements irregular.

In the bitter school of endurance and denial, no house has known the luxury of paint or repair. The buildings stand in drabness and wait for an eventual day of glory.

For the animal with the voice, for the exemplary citizen of the Reich, this hope was still as certain as the glow at the end of their bad cigars. For the citizens it was otherwise.

In the leaden wetness of the hour, the gables of the city below looked like hundreds of half-opened black umbrellas. Here and there, people walked home with the long shadows of street lamps swimming about them. But for most of those at home—the women, the old men, for the unbelievers—hope had run away like a thief in the night. They sat alone in their cold rooms, tight-lipped lest the doubt and fear and despair that ran furiously through their brains, like a thousand squirrels in cages, should spill into the street.

The poet looked down at the bridge. The stone buttresses stood in the surging waters and were like ships going upstream. He counted the slow-moving luminous string of red beads formed by the tail lights of an endless string of trucks that ran over the bridge and lost itself at a curve near Reinhausen. At the side of the bridge, an isolated red light appeared, and when he found it in his binoculars, he congratulated himself.

The light was on the Island, sheltered by the house and the barn. The goose was cooked. The Japanese paper lantern was lit. The distance and the bad light made it difficult to identify anyone. People were half outlined as they stood toward the light. The rest was one with the night, the faces undistinguishable pale disks. They kept moving in and out of the house. He thought he saw four, then five, then six.

The moon came to his aid. It flooded the Danube with light. He saw a figure moving. A man walked from the willows up to the house. It was an old man. The Assessor picked up the phone and called the Gauleiter. Herr Unruh shook with excitement as he talked.

The whirring started again. The wires strained and the tower began trembling. It was seven and the poet held his ears.

Below, the Gauleiter took his pistol and put it into the right outside pocket of his coat. He walked to the tower and on the way up, he rested several times, holding onto the wooden scaffolding that supports the stairs.

Herr Unruh saluted and handed him the binoculars. "Old Anton at last is back," he said.

"At night, all cats are gray," said the animal with the voice. "I hope that you are right."

The paste-white patches that were the faces of the group of people on the Island were in a ring around the table under the lamp.

"I can't make out how many there are," said the Gauleiter, "but I shall find out. Keep an eye on me."

Herr Stolz went down to the street in haste. He descended with agility as if to the music of a minuet. He ran up to his boat which was made fast with chain and padlock at the Schwimmverein. He rowed out into the Danube toward the fifth arch of the bridge, the same through which the pig had traveled. He pulled the oars into the boat and let it drift silently.

He passed the Island, but it seemed dark and quiet. A faint red glow appeared beneath the piling of house and barn. He took his oars and rowed into the calm part of the Danube, and carefully let his boat ride up on the Island's shore.

He took the chain as if it were a costly, golden necklace, and carefully laid it on the ground. As he stepped from the boat, he sank to his ankles in mud. He recovered his footing among gaseous fumes and to bubbling, sucking sounds. He took a second step forward, crawled to dry land where he wiped his hands on grasses, and stood up. He reached into his coat pocket for the pistol, and walked up the path in the shelter of the willow trees. There was no dog to announce him. He stumbled along toward the red glow. The light outlined a heavy wheelbarrow just before he was on top of it. There he stopped.

The moon smeared the Gauleiter's shadow against the barn. He stood still. He bent forward and listened to a voice and a guitar. A man sang:

> As long as the old mare was on her feet
> Nobody gave her bedding or feed,
> Hollaradi, Hollaradiho, Hollaradiho.
> After she was dead, they stuck a bundle of hay
> Between her teeth so that no one could say
> With lack of respect
> That she died of neglect.

"Yes," whispered the animal with the voice, his face bright and smiling like the moon. "That is Anton Fischer come home!"

Awkwardly the Gauleiter lowered himself into the shadow of the bushes and crept on knees and elbows toward the pump. As he looked up out of the grass, he was as happy as the people who sat around the table in the gardenhouse.

Before him was a feast for a prosecutor. Six people, each with both feet in the concentration camp—the old crows who gave shelter to the fugitive, Anton Fischer; an Aryan girl in forbidden intimacy with a prisoner of war; and the Bishop of Regensburg consorting with seditious elements.

Herr Stolz tasted rare sensations as he got up. He drank the full flavor of his powers, the glorious cool exhilaration of duty well performed. He pinned on himself hero's medals and he already read in bold type:

"Single-handed and practically unarmed, Party member and Gauleiter Hermann Stolz—"

The careful official removed the safety catch on his gun.

CHAPTER

12

LENI had placed a glass with six paper roses on the table.

"I hope it's good. Take the goose away," said Saint Anne, and handed the large platter to her sister.

The Bishop said a short prayer. Leni dipped a gravy ladle into a pot while Anton waved a world of winged creatures away from the paper lantern. The sisters sat down and looked worried.

Everybody wished each other good appetite while old Anton carved the goose. The prisoner uncorked the wine. It was young, green, and ordinary, and a good deal of it came out of the bottle as out of a fountain.

"A good roast goose is a good gift of God," said old Anton, and started to eat.

"This bird is as tender as snow, Mesdames," said the prisoner.

The Bishop's chin was glossy with goose fat. He wiped it with his handkerchief, and the little women felt guilty again because there were no napkins on the table. The crockery was ill-assorted and cracked, and there was only one good glass which the Bishop raised.

"To the day when every table will again be as well set as this, in your land and ours," he said looking at the prisoner. "And to the day when we shall be free men."

They clinked glasses and then there was silence and

everybody ate. Old Anton looked at the plate in front of him. He made a sudden important decision.

"I'll eat mine quickly, all at once, as if I had goose every day," he said, and devoted himself to his portion of the goose.

"This is hardly enough for a full table," apologized Saint Martha.

The pig in the barn grunted and the prisoner laughed.

"There is nothing to laugh about this," said Anton. "We better do away with him soon. One day there will be a census of pigs. A man will come with a paper to fill out. The paper asks a hundred questions and the answer to one of them is that the pig is no longer ours, or that we will be executed if we execute the pig without permission."

"The pig will not be executed," said Leni. "How could you think of eating him? Besides, he doesn't even belong to us."

"That kind of reasoning was good and nice a long time ago," said Anton. "Now we are lean and empty, Leni." He pointed to the bones on his plate. "The only thing that belongs to us is what we have had, what we've eaten, what we have worn, what we have been. The goose warming my stomach now, this minute, makes me happy. That's something to remember. I don't think we'll get much more to remember, pig or no pig."

The Bishop stood up to reach into a pocket for a small flask of white liquor that is made by the Carmelite monks of Regensburg.

The cake was sandy and the coffee made of burnt cereal, some dried figs, and chicory.

The Bishop also had three cigars that were the color of packing paper with thick veins. He took them from a leather case, carefully, as if they were the rarest Havanas. He cut the ends off and passed one to Anton and another to the prisoner. Leaning back, they smoked them with half-closed eyes, and talk of old times began.

The Bishop nodded in the direction of the beer garden.

"I look at it every day on my promenade over the bridge. If you don't come too close from the center of the bridge, it looks the same as it did long ago," he said.

He turned his wide frame toward the prisoner, and for his benefit, he spoke very slowly.

"The maniacs, the heavy-footed apostles, threaten that the only alternative to their costly medicine and glory is Bolshevism. That, my friend, is the purest Mumpitz, invented to frighten people."

"Mumpitz" was the Bishop's favorite word for nonsense.

"In his normal state and when he is not in uniform, the common man here is the perfect pattern after which the whole middle class is cut. To play the small householder is his favorite role. As such, he trims his lawn and mends his fences, he picks up every little piece of paper he drops, pays taxes before they are due, and reports himself for infractions of the various city ordinances that concern him. His motto is, 'Small, but Mine.' He wholly lacks the imagination or the desire to divide that. Nowhere in this world are people less inclined to Communism. I don't know about other places, but I will tell you how once they were happy here. I think of it on Sundays, on the bridge, when I look at the garden; and I wish I could turn that clock back up on the tower.

"Once, at an hour when the church bells of all Regensburg tolled, the bells of the cathedral loud and deep above all the others, they were as happy here as I think man can be on earth. The congregation was, as it is now, mostly made up of children and little black women with their Wachsstöcklein. There were more men in church then. And from the church as they wandered over the bridge to the beer gardens—man, woman, and child— they all arrived with music and happy faces."

"A hundred of them in our little garden, and there were ten gardens like ours in Stadt am Hof alone," Anton Fischer said.

"To the right were the bottling works; to the left, the butcher shop; and then, under a roof decorated with pine branches, was a platform where the beer was drawn. To the right of that was the kitchen with a big window, and, inside, an oven bigger than any you have ever seen. There were ten women cooks standing around the oven, red-faced, screaming, throwing pots, dishing out soup, putting fist-sized dumplings into it. The bill of fare was simple, five or six dishes, and on Sunday, suckling pig, or hare with red cabbage, duck and goose—not your kind of cooking, Frenchman, but right for them. The orchestra played in the shell in front of the beautiful blue Danube."

"It was painted new every year—excuse me, your Grace," said old Anton. "I broke in—I wanted to explain to him how it looked—"

"That's right," said the sisters. "Just as it was, and

Anton had it painted new every year by an artist who came from Munich. It cost a lot of money."

"And it was worth it, and so beautiful that most of the people looked at the painted panorama instead of the real," continued the Bishop.

"The congregation that sat in this beer garden never changed. They were as solid and unmovable as the stones in the Danube bridge. They were heavy people, nothing elegant about them and nothing frivolous. They were like the suits they wore—solid, thick as the felt pads that were under their beer mugs. The cloth strained under their arms and over their paunches. Golden thalers and heavy silver horses jumped on their watch chains when they laughed. They were rough, kindhearted, and honorable. Their noses were red. Their eyes were kind and their mustaches were most of the time crested with the foam of beer. When they turned around to look at something, the whole body had to be moved. I don't say it's an ideal to strive for, but for the kind of people they were, they were sensible, whole, responsible, and, above all, content."

"That's right," confirmed the sisters, looking at each other. "That's how it was."

"People came in and sat down where there was room," said old Anton. "Anywhere. Doctor, lawyer, a baron from his estate, schoolteacher, carpenter, Israelites, Catholics, and even Protestants sat peacefully next to each other."

"It was," said the Bishop, "the place where the good word Gemütlichkeit was invented. It was a democracy, solvent, content, and happy. They were people of small possessions, living in a paradise that anyone could aspire to, in which everyone took the great luxuries of self-respect, time, and security for granted.

"They sat in the garden there almost on top of each other. There was hardly room to walk. Food and drink was served on pewter plates. The brown beer came in heavy gray stone mugs. The waitresses were like the Percherons that dragged the heavy beer wagons through the streets. They took six liter mugs in each hand at one time, or they stacked eight portions of food along the left arm and carried a ninth and tenth in the other hand, yelling to impatient customers, 'Ih kimm shoh. Ih kimm shoh.' They advanced toward the crowd like caissons into battle."

"Yes, so it was," said old Anton. "The concert always took three hours, and as the end of the garden slowly emptied, the waitresses collected the red and white checkered tablecloths and went home. They all owned houses. A man with a green apron came to rake the garden, and then it was most beautiful. The hundred tables were grass green, the four hundred chairs were the same green. The sun shone down through the leaves of the chestnut trees on the gravel and lit up the small stones with a dark green light. Even the sparrows were green, and the man in the green apron was green in six various hues. I wonder how old sparrows get, and if any of them that lived there when we had the beer garden are still there."

"Most probably, and most probably they are the same and talk about the same things," said the Bishop. "It's the only thing that has remained true to us—the sparrows, the green of the chestnut trees, the Danube, and the grass."

The Bishop turned to the Frenchman and took the hand of Saint Anna as he explained:

"I lived in an old house close to the brewery. As a student, my stipend was small and I was always hungry. I grew so fast that my clothes seemed to shrink every time I put them on. I was the biggest student in the Diocese.

"These good ladies fed me, they helped me through school; they took care of me in sickness. Fräulein Anna kept my clothes wearable. She let out the trousers and lengthened the sleeves on my jacket; and Fräulein Martha set plates of good food before me in the warm kitchen when I couldn't get to the Seminary. In midwinter the ice rose on the stone buttresses of the bridge. Snowshovels were of no avail and the bridge was closed. Roast goose then tasted even better than it did tonight. I think I was even more hungry."

"How can anybody cry over a lost beer garden?" said old Anton.

Saint Anna cried behind her rough hands and Saint Martha wiped tears from her eyes with the back of her hand. She forgot the eminence of her visitor. She talked to him as if he were still the lean student:

"Tell them about the Pope, Sepperl," she said between sobs. "That's funny."

"Yes," said old Anton, through his own tears. "Stop crying and listen to the story which the Bishop will tell about the visit to the Holy Father."

The Bishop wiped his own eyes with the handkerchief that had served him as a napkin before.

"Many years ago," he began with a face glazed with the grease that he wiped on his nose and cheeks, "it befell me to escort a distinguished visitor through our city. The visitor was even taller than myself. I was a young priest then, and very nervous and scared because the visitor was a Cardinal and he had come straight from Rome. His name was Count Francis Neuwied. He stepped from his train and looked at me with surprise. In the carriage, on the way to the Bishop's palace, he put me at ease. He said I was unusually tall; and when I told him that I was the tallest priest in Regensburg, he informed me that he was, without a doubt, the biggest in the entire church. The Pope himself had told him so, he said.

" 'When I arrive in Rome for my annual visit,' said the Cardinal, 'the Holy Father sees me privately—I have to wait until the ceremonies are over and the stream of visitors is gone. The Holy Father then sends everybody away, even the Swiss guards—he tells them to go and stand outside the door—and then he picks up his heavy robes and walks down from the throne and says, "Franzl, I want to see whether you are really as tall as you look. Stretch out your arms."

" 'I do as he says, and he runs around under them twice or three times until he is satisfied, and then he talks to me for a while and he walks back up to his throne. I think it's the only fun he has, and all the way home I feel as lonesome as he is.' "

The Bishop lit the insignificant remains of his cigar for the third time. He was puffing hard, and when he had it going he leaned back and folded his hands over his middle, and he asked Anton for a song.

The old man plunked on the guitar, started the song of the mare—he was at the third refrain—and sang:

Hollaradi, Hollaradiho, Hollaradiho.
. . . *so that no one could say*
With lack of respect
That she died of neglect.

Tears of sympathy for the lost beer garden had left the eyes of the young girl clouded. Her hard little hand was in that of the prisoner. Their hands were hidden by the girl's wide skirt.

Leni looked straight ahead into the rosy light that hung like fine rain near the pump. As on the screen of a mediocre cinema, indistinct and lightshot, a face appeared.

It took all of Leni's strength to bring her free hand to the prisoner's arm, to pull his sleeve. He looked at her and smiled.

"Dear, sweet Mother of God—," prayed Leni.

She stared straight ahead and the prisoner followed her eyes.

"If it isn't Herr Fischer," said the Gauleiter, jovially addressing himself to Anton. "Where have you been, Herr Fischer? We've missed you." He waited for an answer.

"You're curiously silent. Sit down, Pfaff," the Gauleiter said to the Bishop, who had risen and began to walk toward him.

He turned sideways facing the Bishop, the gun pointed at him.

"Stand still, Pfaff. Stay where you are."

The Bishop kept walking toward him. The Gauleiter raised the gun and shot into the air.

"I am warning you," he screamed. "Halt! Halt!"

"Run, Anton, run," shouted the prisoner.

The Gauleiter turned. His gun searched for the prisoner. He aimed the gun, but the shot never went off. The pistol fell to the floor together with a spade. The Gauleiter reached for his head. Falling forward, he upset the table, and sank onto his knees. His head was on the seat of a chair; the lower lip hung down loose like that of an old horse. The weight of his body dragged him finally to the ground.

The prisoner said, "I will give myself up."

"They would tear your insides out and put out your eyes, Frenchman. They will beat you with shovels and trample you to death. They'll shoot all your friends," said old Anton. "I am an old man. I'll die easier than you will."

The two women stood together as they always did, dry-eyed and wordless, truly the birds of unhappiness.

"It doesn't matter who takes the blame," said the Bishop. "They will come for all of us."

The red paper lantern burned low. The paper roses that had decorated the table lay beside the dead man, next to his gun, as if someone had thrown a bouquet at him.

"There are seven bullets left," said the prisoner, inspecting the magazine of the Mauser.

As they all did, so the prisoner knelt down, but he did not fold his hands. They hung limp at his sides. He looked with open curiosity at the face of the Gauleiter. A thin line of blood ran down the forehead. It stopped and collected at the side of the nose. When the pool filled the eyesocket and came to the height of the cheekbone, it spilled over and dripped down. The lower lip of the dead man was stuck out. It looked as if he was drinking his own blood.

The prisoner suddenly got up. He righted the table, placed the gun on it, and then, with Gallic gestures of impatience, as if he were a neglected customer in a store, tired of waiting and complaining to the management, he said:

"Do something—and make haste."

He pointed upward.

"They know me up there, Paul Laprade, soldier of France, and stretcher bearer number 82 from Lourdes, but they know you better. You're nearer the throne, you're a good man. Pray, Bishop, pray for yourself and for those poor windy souls there, shaking in their old hides, for him, and for the blameless child. Do something. Ask for a miracle. Anyway, try. What good is it to be a Bishop? I don't ask for anything big, nothing elaborate—no visions—no grotto."

He pointed at the dead Gauleiter.

"I'll be satisfied if another one of these comes and takes the gun there and shoots us one after the other. I'll call that miracle enough—"

He held one hand in the other and looked at the Bishop.

"Bishop," said Saint Anna, and she looked at the prisoner, "absolve him."

"Yes," they all said, "absolve him of his sins."

"If the death of the Gauleiter happened in self-defense,"

said the Bishop, "in that case, there is no sin—and therefore no need of absolution. If it was not completely justified, after sincere confession of sin and evidence given of sorrow, then I could absolve him. I have no power beyond that, and, as for miracles, I believe this unhappy earth is too defiled to bear them."

He looked over to his church and at that moment the sirens began to howl. The alarm bells rang, and over their clamor came the "boong, boong" of the bells of the cathedral and all the churches.

"I did not know we were as important as that," said the prisoner.

"It's for the Bishop," answered old Anton. "He's big game for them. They know how to put on a show."

CHAPTER

13

THE poet leaned over the edge of his tower. His neck and arms were motionless, holding the binoculars. He had not taken his eyes off the Island since the Gauleiter's boat arrived there and he became bored. He had followed the dark figure up to the pump, and then he watched it advance to the light. As the Gauleiter's gun went off, Herr Unruh was relieved and satisfied. He put down the glasses and with great importance took the telephone from its box. He asked for Headquarters. The exchange was busy; he yelled into the phone. His voice was drowned in the whining of alarm sirens, and the ringing of all the bells in the city.

He tried again, believing at first that it was a celebration, that the Russians had capitulated, or that some other major victory had been announced.

"I must speak to Headquarters immediately. It is a matter of greatest urgency," he said.

"Attention, attention—air attack, take cover," the telephone answered.

He cursed and jangled the receiver. Now he believed that an unannounced drill was taking place. He picked up his glasses again and searched the sky impatiently.

"It is not possible. It cannot be," he said to himself, and then suddenly left his mouth open. He had seen the first of the attacking planes.

"But, it's impossible. It cannot be," he said several times more.

But, in spite of the poet's doubts, it started, as if the shot fired by the Gauleiter on the Island in the Danube had been the opening signal for the attack.

They came from the direction of Reinhausen. They were harassed and bitterly fought on all sides and they had suffered losses, but they came on steadily, inevitably, as if they were committed to riding rails hung high in the sky.

Unruh studied their sizes and markings. He was trained to believe nothing that he did not see, and, at the same time, to take for fact everything that his superiors told him. On that account there was great upset in his mind. He saw the planes and at the same time disbelieved their existence, because he had been told they would never come. Herr Unruh was, for a while, uneasy in thought.

The soft, distant purring of the air fleet increased to deafening doomsday music which drowned the din of the alarmed city as they came overhead. Across the river the roof of the town hall in Reinhausen exploded. Fiery sleet rose in the air. A second later, the burning shingles of the first house that was hit in Stadt am Hof sailed away like the plumage of a golden bird, and in the new red glow the shining bellies of the planes were overhead.

The open black and red mouths of the Messerschmitt works spewed sheaves of fire as they swallowed the bombs. In the stockyard of the abattoir next to the exploding gasoline and petroleum storage tanks thin Belgian cattle glowed as the hair on their skins ignited, and, a moment after, they were roasted on the hoof.

The districts of Regensburg, Stadt am Hof, and Reinhausen were alight. The superfluous half-moon hung like a yellow hat in a bright room, and the white Walhalla in its forest and the chalk cliffs near the Danube seemed like a picture hanging on the wall. A burning door careened down from one of the bombers. It fell into the Danube.

In perfect discipline of man and machine, the attacker left, following the Danube into the night.

The ancient clock in the bridgetower tried to do its duty. The pendulum swung, the drum began to turn, and the wires strained to lift the hammers overhead to toll the unhappy hour for the citizens of Regensburg.

The poet's head was pushed against a rafter. He dropped the telephone and held onto the balustrade with both hands. He thought that he heard someone whispering and hissing. There was a yammering in the woodwork and then he saw flames beneath him.

The fractured timberwork of the tower collapsed. The floor of planks on which he stood gave way and spilled him. He began to fall, shoulders first. The bells came down after him. Near the bottom of the tower, over the vaulted stone work, the falling timber stacked itself in disorder. The rim of the big hour bell caught him. Gulping helplessly like a fish on dry land, he lay sprawled over a beam. As it cut him from life, the dentated wheel of the clock sank into his shoulders.

He rested, as in a hammock; the uniform held him together, his severed legs dangling down off the beam. The seat of his uniform trousers bulged slowly and began to discolor, and then oozed and dripped like an old coffee-

bag. The boots, which were too large in the shafts, filled with the liquids of his body and fell down into the flames. He bleated for a second. His well-conditioned donkey mind for the last time projected the picture of his idol before him, and, babbling its name, he died.

Smoke rose from the city. From the petroleum and gasoline storage tanks voluptuous brown and black clouds of velvety texture wallowed over the city toward the spires of the cathedral. The bridge was hit in four places. One bomb had landed on the Island in the Danube. The arbor stood at an angle. The wheelbarrow had been thrown into the air and was in pieces, and the staves of an empty beer barrel were blasted from their metal bands; but no one on the Island was hurt.

In the first dawn light, old Anton walked up to the tip of the Island to look at his city.

The bridgetower was like a tall oven, its windows red, smoke pouring from the top. The third arch was damaged, but the bridge and tower stood there as they had always done. The outline of the beloved city was still the same.

Old Anton was glad that he was still here. He went back and sat down with the others in front of the pump. Saint Anna had gone to make some coffee. They all sat in silence on the bench near the pump, old Anton as usual with his back turned. They all took coffee and Saint Martha walked down to the radish plots.

Swallows shot over the Island, hunting the small flies that hovered over the vegetation and the uprooted radishes. They sailed out over the dark water of the Danube, and, lowering their forked tail feathers, quickly sank down to the water to bathe, dipped their long blue-black wings alternately, dragged their bodies, stuck their broad chests and heads into the current, and, again in flight, shook themselves dry. They landed on the telephone wires overhead, where they chirped and straightened out their feathers.

"I wonder how it is," said the prisoner, "when one is terribly rich and able to go anywhere, like those birds. They are training now to go to Egypt for the winter.

"Yesterday it was almost like home. How quick things change. Yesterday I felt happy for a while—"

"So did I," said Anton.

"—when the Bishop talked of the beer garden and the sparrows. Well, they're still true to us, the birds and the grass. In half an hour, when the sun comes up, pretending that nothing has happened, it will be as green as it was yesterday—the sun that is now where? India? America? Japan? There, look! There she is—the free, the godly sun!"

They sat still again, until the first gray light came, until the sun shone briefly between the horizon and a blanket of black clouds. The thin sour whistle of the excursion train that runs from Regensburg to the Walhalla whined as the small engine rounded the curves in the narrow streets of Stadt am Hof. It became visible from time to time, with all its lights on, as it passed beyond the buildings of Reinhausen.

On its side were several hastily painted red crosses and it was filled with stretcher cases and nurses, and it went very slow. It was headed for the Walhalla.

"It's like the trains that came to Lourdes," said the

prisoner. "It fills me with homesickness. I always liked to
go to the trains—"

He sat awhile and thought. The sun was in the smoke
clouds; it was dark again, almost as dark as night. After a
pause, the prisoner talked again:

"One day at nine-thirty the express with the blue cars
and the first-class pilgrims arrived in Lourdes, and it was
more crowded than ever. There were not enough ambu-
lances to take them to their hotels. The train remained
only a few minutes in the station, and, in consequence,
as we always did under such circumstances, we took the
stretcher cases out of the train and placed them on the
ground by the side of the express, over the tracks of
the local train.

"On the day of which I now speak, we had placed a
dozen stretchers over the tracks, and we were climbing
back into the train for more patients when suddenly the
air was filled with the most pitiful screams of agony. We
looked out of the windows of the express train and observed that the cries came from the poor, abandoned pilgrims lying helpless on their stretchers over the rails.
Unexpectedly, a local train was coming down the track
and almost upon them. Then the miracle happened.
When the train was only a few feet away, they were suddenly cured, every one of them. They got off their stretchers and ran."

"And we are sitting here waiting for that train," said
old Anton. "Yes, we are sitting here like the birds on the
telephone wire there, waiting for somebody to come and
shoot us. Even you, Frenchman. Even you've caught the
German illness. We sit here and talk courageously, as if

we were in the American dentist's room, across the river there, waiting to have our teeth painlessly pulled. We are going to wait until they come and ask us questions, and then we will answer them, and they will do what they think is right and proper. It's all right for me—I'm a German. And what did Goethe say again? 'Order is the citizen's first duty.' I have at last achieved the ideal, Frenchman, but you—"

The prisoner got up and walked away. Saint Martha came from the garden with hands folded.

"My poor radishes," she said, and sat down and cried.

"Good God in Heaven, how can you cry about a few radishes at a time like this?" said Anton.

"Let us thank God on our knees that we are still alive," said Saint Anna.

"It might have been better if the bomb had dropped on us and ended it," said Saint Martha.

With sickening suddenness the dead Gauleiter was back among them. He still lay where he had fallen.

"Why didn't it kill him?" said old Anton. "Why didn't one of those bombs fall on him?"

The sun rose out of the smoke. The lightning rods on the spires of the cathedral were aflame like golden swords.

The prisoner stood at the side of the dead man, and then he walked over to the bomb crater. He stood for a while looking at it, with his hands hanging down. Suddenly he came to life and ran back to the others.

"It has happened," he said, "the miracle—it happened last night! We are safe, all of us!" He pointed at the crater. "There it is," he said; "that is the miracle."

"I see no evidence of one," answered the Bishop.

He looked at the prisoner with embarrassment.

"Hear me out. Let the experienced stretcher bearer carry you to safety. We have little time."

The Bishop took a cup of coffee from Saint Anna's hand. He drank slowly from it; his eyes over the rim of the cup looked at the prisoner.

"It's our only hope of life."

"What is?"

"To complete the miracle."

"That's blasphemy," said the Bishop. "I forbid you to talk like a heathen."

"Dear Father, good, honest man, it was all arranged— it was meant that you should choose me of all prisoners. I who know of miracles, I who know that not only the grottoes are sacred, but that every foot of God's earth is miraculous."

"You have fooled me," said the Bishop. "You are not a religious man at all."

"Let a heathen save you then," said the prisoner, "and save himself."

"And how will you do that?" asked the Bishop.

"I have no time to explain, dear Father. The train is almost upon us now, and only half of the miracle is performed. We shall have to do the rest and do it quickly."

The prisoner tapped old Anton on the shoulder and pointed at the Gauleiter.

"You take the feet," he said. "I will take the shoulders."

The body was hard to move. They dragged it to the edge of the bomb crater. It rolled to the bottom itself, leaving the imprint of the oversimple face in the loam as it turned.

The prisoner called to old Anton and told him to row the Bishop across the Danube to Reinhausen and then to go and inform the authorities of the Gauleiter's death.

"I must ask you to let me finish this alone. He is too whole. He looks as if he had died in bed. They're all professionals. They know better how the dead should look than anyone else on earth. I've seen their work.

"Here then. dear Father, we say farewell."

He turned. He ran to the barn, took a can of kerosene, an ax, the shovel, the Gauleiter's gun, and went back to the bomb crater. He was up to his knees in stagnant water. It was hard to begin. He thought awhile of his home, then suddenly he raised the spade. "This is for my mother," he said, as the shovel came down—

"And this is for my father"; and when he had ended, he threw the broken wheelbarrow into the ditch and covered his tracks.

He studied the arrangement for a while. "It's like the souvenirs they've left everywhere—exactly so," he said.

He was satisfied and went down to the Danube. He wanted to wash his hands and his face, but he fell to earth as a man who has come upon water in the desert. He crawled to the edge. Finches chirped and small fishes shot away. He bent, looked at himself, and became ill.

They came in two boats, in full regalia and with boots on. They marched up the path and Leni pointed the bomb crater out to them.

"That should be the Gauleiter Stolz?" said the Gruppenführer Schuft doubtfully.

"Ta, ta, ta, that's him," said a Party member who identified the Gauleiter by tailor's markings and papers.

They stood for a while, looked at each other, and were glad that they were all there and not as the Gauleiter. They swallowed and pulled on their tunics and made callous, soldierly remarks about war and death.

The shouting Gruppenführer brought order into the group. Hands were slapped on the trouser seams, buttocks were pressed together, eyes to the front. The group stood at attention as at the side of an open grave. Herr Schuft ordered a salute and a song. He spoke movingly of the dead comrade's noble example, Party loyalty, devotion to Führer and Fatherland; he deplored the irreparable loss of the Gauleiter.

Herr Schuft left an honor guard of two men while he marched off and had himself rowed over to the Blue Danube where he and his companions washed peculiar feelings from their insides with several seidels of beer and discussed the changes that were needed since the Gauleiter's demise.

Frau Stolz, informed by the police, walked into her shop and opened a drawer. For once, a German widow had enough black-bordered handkerchiefs to dry her tears.

C H A P T E R
14

THE next day was Sunday, and the prisoner helped the two old sisters and Leni into the boat and rowed them ashore. The Strudel was whiter than usual. The wind howled in the arches of the bridge. They climbed out of the pitching boat and walked up the quay, past the Gauleiter's house, and toward the cathedral. First only their own boots—and those of the Gauleiter's wife—clattered along over the cobblestoned streets, but then from everywhere people came, walking toward the cathedral.

The side door of the church was opened, and the Bishop's small, dewy garden was filled with people waiting to squeeze into the vast cathedral. Saint Martha and Saint Anna kneeled in prayer. An old priest followed the coughing sacristan to a small altar in one of the side niches. He started to celebrate Low Mass. The Gauleiter's wife had unwound her candle, and she said prayers for the soul of her dead husband; she gave tearful thanks to God for the drab, hopeless life that had been as dark and unrelieved as the clothes she wore. Beside her knelt the maid and cried.

The Bishop walked into the crowded cathedral. The mass was at its beginning. He climbed the circular stone steps to the choir, sat down at the organ, and pulled all the stops. Through the immense structure surged a storm of music, a roar as wild as the sound of the Danube under

the fifth arch of the bridge. As if wine were poured into goblets, the carmine and ocher east windows of the vast structure began to glow in the sunrise, and as the people left the cathedral, the new day was waiting outside. The sky was the simple blue of paint on children's blocks. Below, on the river, the prisoner had sat on a stone bench along the quay waiting for the women.

Soldiers were removing casualties from a bombed building. The prisoner watched all this, shook his head. "Look at them," he said aloud to himself, "they march even when they carry stretchers." His Gallic temper ran away with him. As if he were in a village street in France, he shouted, "You, Sergeant, you can't do that—you can't let them carry a sick man like that. You must be out of step when you carry a man on a stretcher, so that he is comfortable. If you march, hup, hup, hup, you shake the intestines out of him—you kill him!"

The sergeant was far behind his men. "That's true," he said, "but we have no command for marching out of step."

"Oh, but that's easy. Invent one. Just say, 'Out of step, march!' "

The sergeant tried it out. "It works," he said.

"All you have to do," said the prisoner, "is to yell at them."

It was then that the sergeant came to his senses and found that he had been ordered about by a prisoner of war. "You shall hear of this," he said, and ran after the stretcher bearers.

"Whoever is their master must shout at them—in the beginning, anyway," thought the prisoner.

He rowed the people back to the Island.

"I don't care," said old Anton, "there's a new air blowing. I feel like another man."

He left Leni and the Frenchman under the Apostle trees. They sat at the edge of the Island, with their feet in the Danube in plain view of the bridgetower.

The mechanism that was set for a thousand years was silent.

"The clock is gone, and the sun is hiding her face, but my stomach tells me that it's close to noon. I'm going to my beer garden," said old Anton. He walked into the house and reached for a leather bag, and dug deep down in it for a handful of coins, and he took his hat from a nail.

"Anton, stay here," said Saint Anna. "You shouldn't even walk around the Island; you should hide in the daytime."

He shook his head. He said, "Don't worry about me."

"Anton," said Saint Martha, "you're getting fresh again. Be careful."

He bent down as if to make exercises, jingled the coins in his pocket, and pressed the hat down on his head. And on the way to the boat, he picked up two radishes. He crossed the river to Reinhausen, and, standing up, punted upstream on the other side until he was in front of the beer garden. He waved at Frau Saltner from his boat, made it fast, and ran up the steps and around to the entrance of the Blue Danube.

When she saw him come through the passage, the old woman screamed, "Ja, Herr Fischer, where do you come from? I couldn't believe my eyes when I saw you—you've got your young legs under you. Let me touch you. Ja wie gehts denn?"

"Mir gehts wunderbar, Frau Saltner."

"Herr Fischer," she said, "confidentially, I have to tell you, I don't know what's the matter with me, but I feel different since it happened—altogether different. I am a new woman."

"I know, Frau Saltner."

"I was scared while the bombing was going on, but after I began to feel calm—and peaceful—very peaceful— as I haven't for years. I can't help it, Herr Fischer. I breathe easier from all the way down here in my chest. I don't suppose it's right to say that."

"You can say it to me."

"So you're back. I always said you'd come back, Herr Fischer, and you came back just in time for the funeral. What shall it be, Herr Fischer?"

"Salt, bread, and beer, Frau Saltner. I saved two radishes—one for you, one for me."

She placed a plate, a knife, a basket of black bread, and a salt cellar before him, and he made himself comfortable.

Frau Saltner brought him his beer, and sat down with him. The radishes began to cry. "How quickly things happen. A week ago, sitting at this table here, Gauleiter Stolz complained about the Government. He's the only one I have ever heard complaining about anything in a loud voice. He said the regulations forbade the sale of mourning apparel, as it was forbidden to show any outward sign of grief. And he cried because he was stuck with black crepe and black-bordered handkerchiefs."

"And now he's dead," said old Anton.

"Yes—and the Party funerals aren't any more what they used to be. Only yesterday new regulations went into effect. For once," said Frau Saltner, "I'm complying. I'm not showing any outward or any inward sign either. Look, Herr Fischer, there they come. My God, he's all alone—a horse, a wagon—not even the widow."

"Since yesterday funerals have been forbidden altogether. I'm surprised they allowed him even a coffin," said old Anton.

"Well, you know why—because he's a Gauleiter. And look—what's left of the Assessor Unruh must be in that black box," said Frau Saltner. She sat down with old Anton and kept looking at the bridge. "God in Heaven," she said, "what's that? Look, Herr Fischer. A joke is a joke, but that's too much."

A man, the only person who followed the coffin and the box, passed over the bridge. He was in a blue suit, but his hands and face were blackened.

"Well, everyone in his own fashion," said old Anton. "He's not allowed to wear a dark suit, or even a black band on his arm, nor a top hat, or even to have a priest. So the only friend the Gauleiter has blackens his face and his hands to show his grief—a rebel of a sort, a man of courage, Frau Saltner. I am too old to be surprised by anything any more. I think it's exactly as it should be."

"Herr Fischer, you'll get in trouble if you don't keep quiet. You're hardly out of it. You know what I think, Herr Fischer? I wouldn't say that to anybody else, but I believe you started all this.

"Tell me how you did it, Herr Fischer. 'How did he do it?'—that's what I always say to people when I tell the story. How did old Fischer get the courage? He's not like that at all. In all the years I knew him he was a quiet man, never raised his voice," said Frau Saltner. "Tell me how you did it." The procession was half-way over the bridge.

"Oh, before I decided to do it," said old Anton, looking over at the hearse, "I had to get very mad—and that doesn't happen to me easily. My stomach turned several times, and then I became very quiet, but while I talked to him I suddenly knew what I had to do. I knew that I would hit him and I knew just where I was going to hit him, and I walked slowly—you remember, Frau Saltner? Well, you remember I sat here." Old Anton sat down on the chair on which he had sat that Sunday noon. "Here I sat, like this, and the Gauleiter was where you are now, and then I said to him what I had to say, and I walked over here, and by then I was as mad as I ever was in my life, and I took him by the collar—" Old Anton was so excited he smacked Frau Saltner. "That's how I did it, and I wish you wouldn't ask me to tell it."

"I'm sorry," said Frau Saltner. "I don't mind. It was very simple," she said, "the way you told it." She looked after the Gauleiter's funeral. "Well," said Frau Saltner, "that's over."

The Gauleiter's miserable coffin and the Assessor's box, which seemed to slide along over the stone banister of the bridge, were on their way to Reinhausen, faithfully followed by the lone mourner with the blackened face and hands.

"I don't approve of things like that," said Frau Saltner. "Let the dead be. But otherwise, I must admit, I'm glad,

Herr Fischer. I can't say I'm not. Maybe it's a sin to even think it. Just the same, I'm glad he's gone, and I'm glad that the other one is gone, too." She turned around to see if anyone was listening. "Now if a few hundred more like those disappear, we'll be all right."

At the end of the bridge, the wagon with the coffin and the box turned to the right, and the little man with the dark face turned left and ran into the beer garden.

"Jessas, Maria, und Joseph!" cried Frau Saltner, "who are you? Who is that?"

The man with the dark face walked to a table and sat down. He ordered a pint of beer, unconcerned by the disturbance he had caused.

Frau Saltner came close. "My God, it's Herr Oberassessor Nebenzahl," she said. "Look at yourself—how you look, Herr Oberassessor."

The Oberassessor was surprised and shocked. He looked at his hands. His face was smeared with soot, his hands and neck dirty, his suit smudged. He excused himself. His morning, he said, had been filled with glory. He explained that he had been called back to assume his old duties; he was reinstated with full rank. What a day today, he sang. He had entered the building against the advice of the firemen; he could not stay away from his old office. "The disorder, the dirt, is unbelievable!"

While Frau Saltner ran to get a beer for the Herr Oberassessor, he turned to old Anton. "I can't believe it yet, Herr Fischer, but—times are changing. I have been called back to my post by the Herr Burgomaster himself," he explained. "This morning I went to look at my old office, to see what had happened in my absence, and look at me—it's partly the bombing, partly the man who had taken my place. Unruh had the furniture moved. Nothing is where it was."

"Also, where did you get so black, Herr Oberassessor?" said Frau Saltner, as she put the beer down.

The Oberassessor, with a large handkerchief, was smearing the dirt all over his face. "It will take years to clean it up," he said, "to unravel the confusion. The archives are burned out. Some things we will never get in the order again in which they were. The stink of warm glue! The smell of burned leather bindings! Oh, the cabinets and files that represent the best years of my life, in which I have filed away the reports and titles of property. Most of the files from A through XYZ up in flames; all deeds, tax records, tax receipts, practically from the year one up to now—carbonized. It will take me twenty years—the rest of my life—to bring order into it."

"What will happen, Herr Oberassessor?"

"I have an excellent memory, but it's going to be terrible just the same. I have a suspicion, Herr Fischer, that many properties will find themselves with owners that cannot prove their titles, and vice versa."

"And what about those you can't remember about?"

"Oh, fiscally speaking, Herr Fischer, these properties will look for their owners, like lost dogs wandering around and searching for their masters. And when finally the dog has sniffed on a lot of shoes and found his lost master's trouser cuff, when he sits up and offers a paw and enough decent people say, 'Why, yes, I remember that was his dog—look at it wagging its tail'—then the dog will be yours again."

The cold wind from the Danube played in the chestnut trees, the branches swayed. Old man Fischer pointed upward and pulled Nebenzahl's ear. "Look up, Herr Oberassessor. My dogs are already wagging their tails. Frau Saltner, today is a wonderful day. We'll drink to the future—a liter for each of us, and for the musicians, and one for you, Frau Saltner."

The beer came, they stood up, and the orchestra that had now shrunk to a guitar and a zither played:

> *Hoch soll er leben,*
> *Hoch soll er leben,*
> *Dreimal Hoch.*

They ate the radishes and the Oberassessor paid for the next round.

It was twelve-thirty. Frau Saltner got up from the table and waited on a group of people that came into the beer garden.

At one-thirty-two, Captain Trost, the fine man from Dachau, in his slim black coat and the cap with the silver skull and bones, stepped from the Munich Express, strode through the railroad station, and proceeded to the city hall. He marched to room number 51, and after he had entered he was saluted by the man behind the desk with a degree of sloppiness that the captain had never before suspected in this official. He was handed the usual pack of envelopes, without greeting or comment.

"How many today?" he asked.

"Count them," said the man behind the desk.

"Only six?"

"Why only six? Don't you read the papers, Captain? We were bombed yesterday, we lost several men. Incidentally, this is my last day in this office. I have been appointed the new Gauleiter of Regensburg—that was in the paper also this morning."

The captain understood immediately. Every muscle in his body stiffened, he came to his most rigid attention, he faced the Gauleiter, saluted, and remained frozen in alert and respectful stance while the Gauleiter relaxed. He had his hands on the armrests of his swivel chair, and, leaning back in all directions, turning the chair to every angle possible, he drank in glory. He let the fine man from Dachau exert himself for several minutes, and when all was said that could be said about the Fatherland, the Führer, the Party, the dead Gauleiter and the living one, Herr Schuft stretched himself in his new tunic and, offering his hand to the captain, got up and put him at ease with the offer of a cigarette, the assurance of his esteem for the Black Corps, and particularly the man who embodied its ideals so well in the person that stood before him. After a solemn second handshake, a look into each other's eyes, and a snappy salute on both sides of the desk, the ceremony was ended.

The captain opened his collar and stepped to the window while the new Gauleiter sat down again.

Complete harmony and equilibrium had been established. With the newly found nonchalance that equality in rank allowed them, with gestures and a tone of voice impossible a minute ago but wholly in order now, the captain in turn offered the Gauleiter a cigarette, lit it for him, drew back the wide black cuff of his left sleeve, pushed the glove up on his hand, and looked at his wristwatch.

He told the Gauleiter that he had nothing to do for the next three hours, and Gauleiter Schuft offered himself as guide. As he always did, so now Captain Trost lifted the embroidered flap of the side pocket on his greatcoat, stuck the six small manila envelopes into the pocket, smoothed down the flap, and then, slapping his hip, smoothed the bulge. Together they descended the stairs of the city hall and walked up on the stone bridge, from where the damage done to the city could best be estimated.

Four diagonal pillars of smoke supported the ceiling of dust-laden clouds that scraped against the crosses of the cathedral. Fanned by the cold wind, flames reflected themselves in the indigo-colored Danube. The new Gauleiter gave his guest an estimate of the damage done and identified the targets that were hit and those missed.

Respectfully the captain walked on the pavement while the Gauleiter walked at his right on the narrow sidewalk. They crossed over the rest of the bridge and to the Blue Danube. The jovial Gauleiter pointed at the ivy-framed passage that led into the beer garden and invited his new comrade to a glass of beer.

It was late when they arrived. The Blue Danube was filled with the small people who frequented it on Sunday afternoons. Everybody had been served, and those who wanted more beer got up and got it themselves.

The occupants of the table at which the Gauleiter and his guest sat down had moved to be closer to the table at which the Oberassessor and Anton sat with Frau Saltner. The old man had borrowed the guitar from the orchestra and was singing, and his audience sat in a close circle around him.

On the table in front of the Gauleiter were several empty beer glasses and a dirty ashtray. They hung their caps on the tree nearest to them, sat down, and the captain took his gloves off.

"Very quaint here," he said. They listened to the singing for a while and then the captain leaned toward the Gauleiter and asked: "Who is that singing?"

"I just wanted to tell you," said the new Gauleiter. "You have him in your pocket there. His name is on one of the envelopes I gave you."

"Oh!" said the fine man from Dachau.

"Yes," said the Gauleiter.

After the song was ended, Frau Saltner said to old Anton, "Can you imagine, Herr Fischer, how beautiful it will be when you can sit here, and open your mouth again and say what you please, without first turning around to look who is listening—when you can talk without lowering your voice!"

The edge of a knife clinked against an empty beer glass.

Frau Saltner took her arm from the back of Anton's chair and turned. She got up and walked to the Gauleiter's table and took the order.

Anton was drowsy. He had not noticed her going. He put the guitar down. "Ah," he said, "it will be like washing yourself, like putting on a clean shirt. It will be a bath for the soul, in cool water, a bath in the Strudel."

What followed should have come from the mouths of people like old Anton, but it was said by the fine man from Dachau. The muscles that bring the lower jaw up against the upper tightened in his face, they played beneath his cheeks for a while. His eyes stabbed into those of Gauleiter Schuft as he said:

"Arrest, arrest, arrest; to survive we must be merciless, vigilant night and day. We must not only be satisfied with man as he is, but know what he has been, and who his friends are. We don't want turncoats, converts, or dreamers. We must comb the lice out of our pelts with the sharpest comb there is. They must go. Not a whisper must pass your ears unnoticed, not a cryout of anyone; the smallest complaint must make you suspicious. You must learn to know them by looking at them; you must hear their thinking. They must be dragged out of hiding and found, no matter how they are disguised. It is they or us. Those who are with us are our brothers, and for the others we shall build abattoirs in every city in the land."

"You speak like the printed book," said the new Gauleiter.

They drank their beer.

"Who is the man with him?"

"That is Oberassessor Nebenzahl; you shall get him later. First he must do some work for us."

Gauleiter Schuft paid, and the legs of the metal chairs scraped in the sand as they got up. They walked slowly through the garden. As they came to the table at which Anton sat, the fine man from Dachau stopped. He looked at Anton with interest, as if the old man's face appeared on a stamp he was about to paste in his album.

The captain turned toward the crowd. He looked from face to face. All careless postures changed, glasses were placed on the tables, the arms taken from women's shoulders. No one stretched himself or yawned. All talk stopped. Only the sparrows' arguments continued under the tables.

All was well. The ancient illness was there with its tearful symptoms evident in every face. The untouchables with their honorable faces looked down into their beer or at their hands. They sat orderly and silently in their shabby clothes, in the position they had learned in school when they were small children—the feet together, the hands on the table. The fine man from Dachau left. He was satisfied.

Two men wearing armbands came into the beer garden. One of them carried a metal canister, solidly constructed for permanent use, equipped with a padlock, a handle, and a funnel that was ingeniously designed so that the man who held the can could see the size and denomination of the coin that was inserted. The cans were in use the year round. This day the collection was dedicated to the bombed-out Regensburgers. The system of collection, well rehearsed and tried out, was simple: On the street it consisted of confronting people, obstructing their passage, taking rather than asking. The collector stuck the can out at the height of his chest, almost touching the donor's; he shouted the slogan of the day, such as "Winterhilfe"; the donor brought out his coin, which was inserted; the donor was given a small emblem to stick on his lapel; the Party greeting followed; the transaction was over. The second man added importance, saw that no one got by without contributing, and changed roles with his partner, when that one's arm got lame.

In beer gardens, the manual recommended equally effective methods. One of the collectors remained at the exit to discourage anyone's leaving, while the other went from table to table.

Everyone had contributed. The collection was heavy. The two men sat down near the exit of the beer garden; Frau Saltner brought them each a free beer and a plate of food.

"The only one that will make any trouble here," said one collector to the other, "is this old woman. We better wait until she goes into the house. It will be easier then."

A shaft of sunlight fell on the trees. The thin ribs in the chestnut leaves glowed like the wires in light bulbs. It was the loveliest hour in the beer garden—the dusty green glow was on every stone, it hopped with the sparrows, it was in the beer glasses, it was along the stakes of the fence, and the trunks of the trees were wrapped in it.

Frau Saltner picked up the glasses of the departed officials and walked into the house. The two collectors wiped their mouths and got up. They walked through the garden, to Anton. One of them tapped him on the shoulder, bent down to him, and said, "Come with us, quietly, and without causing any disturbance." The other picked up the guitar and placed it on Frau Saltner's chair.

Old Anton turned and looked at the crowd, but their faces were averted. They sat as if the man from Dachau was still watching them. Anton looked over his shoulder at the men standing behind his chair, and his tongue was heavy. After a while he said, "Ja, ja, Ih kimm shoh!" He looked for his hat. One of the men gave it to him. They lifted him from the chair, almost with tenderness, and supported him while he tried to stand. He looked around a third time, as if he wanted to say good-by to somebody. He looked for Frau Saltner but she was not there, and one of the men said: "Come, now."

They took him through the garden. Nobody moved, no hand was raised, no one said a word, no one came to his aid. When they were out of sight, in the underpass, the old man came to life. He cursed them, he suddenly jerked himself away and ran. One of the two put the collection can down, the other ran and laughed, like boys playing a game. They caught him in a corner and they took him into the Sunday evening emptiness of the cobbled square outside the beer garden. One of them held him, while the other unlocked the door of the van. They lifted him up and put him in, closed the door, and hung the heavy lock on it. One drove, and the other, with the collection canister in his lap, turned the handle of the siren.

The old man jumped for a while against the four walls of the vehicle, like a bird in a cage, and threw his shoulder against the door, but then he became prudent. He heard the Danube. He had always seen his beloved city in the wide frame of the free man; now it appeared in the ten-by-twenty-centimeter opening of a barred window. His face was like that of a little old monkey in a zoo, his eyebrows pulled up into his wrinkled forehead. He pressed his cheek against the opening and held his head sideways to see. The worn banister of the stone bridge ran outside like an endless ribbon; below, the swallows sat along the telephone wire. The Island appeared, and the Apostle trees. Saint Anna and Saint Martha stood together at the end, near the Strudel, waiting for him. Little Leni, with hands folded, was beside the pump, and the obligatory twenty feet away from her stood the prisoner, and smoke came from the chimney of the house.

The van slowed down and it became dark inside. The car passed through the base of the tower and into the narrow streets. He sank back onto the wooden bench and put his hands against his face. He was hot; his thin shirt, his threadbare coat, were moist. He slapped his knees, and slapped his knees again. He looked intently at the black ceiling of the rolling car, as if that alone would open it, and he searched in vain in all his pockets and in all the corners of the car for a weapon.

The river played with the reflections of the gray-blue bridge, distorted the dark cathedral; the towers and the houses swayed in the waters and were pulled to one side and swam back again. The lightning rods and crosses in the sky glowed, and the Walhalla blushed again as the sun sank.

Frau Saltner collected the tablecloths and then tilted the tables, raising one end by placing a folded metal chair under it, so that rain during the night would run off. The leaves of the chestnut trees hung like wet washcloths from their branches, and the halfwit with the green apron folded the metal chairs, placed them into rows, and then raked the sand. Slowly, the shapes of the tree trunks began to wander away in the darkness.

Near the orchestra shell stood a group of people, Regensburg's handful of so-called "good Germans." Some of them wept. The nostalgic beggars, the gentle members of churches and libraries, the patient civil servants, the good householders, the disciplined professionals, signers of deeds and small mortgages, the forever common, forever honest common man, the frugal dreamers, their little hopes ambushed and surrounded—they stood together under the trees like cattle in the rain, patients waiting for the white-coated attendants to take them back into the asylum.

"Go home," said Frau Saltner. "Why don't you go home?" But they waited; they stood around until Frau Saltner told her old story again—and they listened as children do to a wondrous fairy tale.

"Here was old Anton," it began—

The ill ones in the beer garden looked hungry again, and tilted their heads sideways, and afterwards they walked home in the dark. It was evident that if, in the long night in which they lived, any light would come to them, it had to come from the outside—for those within the walls who had courage and spirit were too few, too old, and much too sentimental.

ACROSS from Regensburg on the Danube is a small, remarkable island. Annually it disappears briefly under the not-blue waters of the river, and then reappears, its boundaries changed and strange objects washed ashore. Back to it then come the Fischers, Anton, his two old sisters, and Leni, their niece, who are the only inhabitants of the island. Once again they plant the seeds of the wonderful big white beer radishes which they sell to the beer garden in Regensburg.

To the immense distress of the Ober-assessor of Regensburg, the island has no legal existence. Various repulsive Regensburg citizens, flourishing under Nazi rule —in particular a Gauleiter and his crony, the official "poet"—resent the Fischers.

Precipitated by an "incident" in the beer garden, the story develops as a war between good and evil. Only Bemelmans could take such ingredients and weave a story that is tender and funny and gay and sad.

The pictures, too, are Bemelmans'. There are fourteen of them, plus the title page, reproduced in full color, and an endpaper.